DANGEROUS TURN AHEAD

Sherri Gallagher

Comfort PUBLISHING

DANGEROUS TURN AHEAD

For information, address Comfort Publishing, 296 Church St. N., Concord, NC 28025. The views expressed in this book are not necessarily those of the publisher.

This book is a work of fiction. Any resemblance to anyone living or dead is purely coincidental.

First printing

Book cover design
by Reed Karriker

ISBN: 978-1-936695-49-2
Published by Comfort Publishing, LLC
www.comfortpublishing.com

Printed in the United States of America

DEDICATION

This book is dedicated to Eagle Scouts everywhere. You demonstrate each and every day that a Scout is trustworthy, loyal, helpful, friendly, courteous, kind, obedience, cheerful, thrifty, brave, clean, and reverent.

I would also like to dedicate this book with my deepest thanks to a true Texas gentleman, my agent, Terry Burns. Thank you to Maureen Lang, Julie Dearyan, Dawn Hill and all the members of the Fremont Christian writers group for guiding my writing to ever better levels in the craft.

Thank you to my husband for getting a bowl of cereal for dinner with a smile because I was so involved in writing a chapter I lost track of time.

Thank you to Mike and Bill Brown, my son, Shane, and all the leaders and members of Troop 198 for their inspiration and antics, that I was able to exaggerate to make this book interesting.

Finally, thank you to all my canine partners; past — Taz and Clara, present — Lektor and Belle, and future, my life is richer for having known you.

CHAPTER 1

Gabe strolled into the lunch room. The aroma of pizza, pop tarts, and hotdogs mingled together with the steam from the serving tables. The faint odor of disinfectant from the overflowing trash cans created that unique smell found only in school cafeterias. Hundreds of students carried on conversations, and the chatter and laughter rose up as the clock ticked down.

He glanced around the brightly lit room and then joined the serving line. His muscles relaxed and he smiled. For once Gabe's clumsy body obeyed his commands.

Then he spotted her watching him.

Confidence flowed from the new clothes he wore today. Yes, he was totally in control. Let her watch him. He'd sit next to her. She didn't need a name, though he knew it was Jasmine. He fantasized about calling her Jazz like her friends did. She was the vision he held onto as he drifted off to sleep each night and each morning he woke up with the hope of finally speaking to her. The knowledge of how little he usually belonged always twisted his tongue into a knot and choked his voice into a crack in his throat but today would be different.

Yes, today would be different!

For his fifteenth birthday recently his parents had given him the biggest surprise — a complete new outfit including the super expensive name brand jeans along with a rock band hoody. Now he fit in. This time he'd get the words out.

"What can I get you, hon?" The black knit hair net was a stark contrast to the lunch lady's white hair. She always wore it with the knot in the middle of her forehead, and a big white apron splattered with the lunch of the day, the usual plastic gloves were on her hands.

"Three hot dogs, please." His mouth watered as the soft, steamed tube steaks were dropped into buns. "Load'em up."

"Same as usual?"

Gabe nodded and the old woman smiled at him and piled chili, onions, relish, and a big squirt of mustard on top. He reached up and grasped the edges of the paper plate lifting it from the top of the clear glass serving area and willed nothing to spill as he lowered it to his tray. A sigh escaped when he succeeded. He pushed the tray down the rails and grabbed a large lemonade.

At the end of the line he waved his ID in front of the scanner and lifted the tray. He glanced around to see if she was still at the same place. Daniel and another boy blocked his path. With his big feet and loaded tray he couldn't get around them.

"Hey, look at the janitor's kid trying to look cool in his nifty new duds. Did your daddy steal them from the lost and found?"

Ignoring them wasn't an option. Past experience demonstrated that path ended with his lunch on the floor and no time nor extra money to buy something else to eat.

"Look guys, just go away and leave me alone. I wasn't bothering you."

"You being here bothers me."

Gabe tried to shoulder his way past, but it didn't work. One of them hit his tray while the other pushed Gabe forward. Mustard smeared his hoody and cold lemonade flowed down his legs in an icy river.

"Ha,ha look the janitor's kid pee'd himself." Daniel laughed and leaned on his buddy.

The other boy pointed. "Yeah-, he's just a big horse so he doesn't know not use the floor for a toilet."

Gabe turned and hurried to the restroom to try and salvage his ruined clothes. He ducked his head to hide the tears in his eyes and tried to ignore the laughter that followed him from the room. A last glance told him she had seen the whole thing and laughed, too.

Maybe he'd just stay in the bathroom for the rest of the day.

CHAPTER 2

"3(5 + 6x) = 51, find X." Gabe read. "Easy." Quickly he punched numbers into his calculator, looked at the screen and wrote down the answer of six. He flipped to the back of the book. He finally had it. He understood the math, now maybe he could pull up his grade.

Running his finger down the page he stopped about half-way to read the answer.

"It can't be. How did they get two?" Gabe rested his head in his hands and stared at the page until the numbers and letters blurred. His stomach hurt.

He might as well tattoo dummy on his forehead. He'd never pass math. Shaking his head, he walked toward the kitchen to grab a soda. Maybe a break would help.

"Corrine, I'm worried about Gabriel," his dad was saying. Gabe stopped walking so abruptly he almost fell. His mother and father had their backs to him. He backed out of the kitchen doorway and flattened himself against the wall to eavesdrop on the conversation.

Gabe heard the oven door close.

"Why, Rich, did the school call?" Mom asked.

Gabe's heart bounced off his shoes because he knew he had a D average, but he really had tried to improve. He knew that he was slow but couldn't they have given him a chance to bring it up before calling?

"No it wasn't the school, but his attitude. Did you see him leave this morning?"

"Yes," she answered, "as a matter of fact I did. That smile was worth every penny that those clothes cost."

"He walked out of here with confidence."

"So what's the problem?"

"When he came home he had a huge mustard stain on his new hoody and I smelled lemonade on his jeans. I'm afraid that someone's bullying him."

"The boy is fifteen years old, over six feet tall and close to two hundred pounds. Who in their right mind would try to bully him? He's growing so fast that he's clumsy. I'll bet he tripped over his own feet and spilled his lunch again. He'll be all right once he stops growing."

Mom's remark drove the air out of his lungs.

Then he realized his father had figured out the truth.

"I don't know which is worse, Mom thinking I'm a klutz or Dad figuring out what really happened," he muttered.

Moving carefully, so as not to make any noise, he back-tracked down the hallway to the safety of his room. Slumping into the desk chair, he replayed the scene from lunch.

"I don't understand why my father's job is important to them. So my dad's a janitor and he wears a uniform and theirs are stockbrokers and wear suits. Dad could've been as good as them if he'd finished college. Why is that their excuse to push me around? All I want to do is hang out, not be class president or make them look up to me," he thought.

"Gabe, is everything okay?"

Straightening, Gabe put a smile on his face and turned to his father, who leaned against the door jam.

"Yeah, everything's fine. I don't get this math homework, that's all."

"Are you sure? You know I'll listen, if you want to talk about anything."

How would he handle a bully? He would probably step in and fix it like Gabe was a baby.

But he wasn't a baby anymore.

"How much math did you do in college?" Gabe asked.

"Not much, I was a marketing major and worked nights as a janitor. No math required and that was over twelve years ago so I don't remember much."

"Why don't you go back to school and finish your degree? I don't need someone home to watch me anymore."

"I'm too close to retiring with a decent pension. If I leave I'll end up with a fraction of that and I'm too old for anyone to hire me into marketing now." His dad straightened to a standing position. "You're changing the subject. Is there something you want to talk about?"

"It's my fault Dad got stuck in a dead end job and I'm not going to make it worse for my parents," Gabe thought.

"Yeah, I'm sure," Gabe answered.

"Supper's ready, then we have to leave for Boy Scouts."

"My homework's not done."

"Bring it along. When it comes to game time you can finish it instead."

Perfect. So much for the most fun part of the evening.

*****

Gabe looked at the new patrol of boys and swallowed hard. They were so little and looked really lost and worried.

"New guys, into room six," Gabe ordered and herded the group in the right direction.

"I'm your patrol guide, and my name is Gabe. Tonight you have to choose a patrol name, a patrol leader, an assistant patrol leader, and start working toward the rank of Tenderfoot."

He leaned back against the wall and watched the boys chatter and argue as they looked through the book of patrol patches. He tried to get a feel for their individual personalities. By the time they came up with the patrol name of Ravens he had a pretty good idea who were the leaders. Could he get the right ones to volunteer for what they did naturally?

"Time to get a patrol leader. Anyone want to step up?" Gabe looked around, hiding his smile. A raised hand would have been a surprise. "Look guys, it's not hard. All you have to do is make sure your patrol has jobs assigned to everyone for the camp outs and to call the patrol with changes in plans."

Still no hands.

"You'll have a list of everybody's number and if you have a problem, you can call me for help," he added.

A dark haired boy named Chuck raised his hand tentatively. "That's all we have to do?"

"Yeah. It's really easy and you need to demonstrate leadership skills if you want to become an Eagle Scout," Gabe answered.

"Okay, I'll try," Chuck said.

Gabe let out a sigh, two items down, one to go. "Now we need an assistant patrol leader. The assistant fills in if the patrol leader can't make it and it counts toward leadership, too."

"Hey, I'd rather be an assistant than a patrol leader," Chuck said.

Gabe couldn't hide his smile, anymore. "Too bad, you already accepted the position. But don't worry patrol leadership changes after each court of honor." Chuck subsided and slumped in his chair.

Two boys, Shane O'Hara and Kevin McConnell raised their hands.

"We need to vote. Everybody close your eyes and put your heads on the table. Those in favor of Shane for assistant patrol leader raise your hands." Gabe took a mental count.

"Those in favor of Kevin as assistant patrol leader raise your hands." Gabe pointed to each hand to make sure he counted correctly.

"Shane is assistant patrol leader."

Kevin sat up. "Wait the vote was equal, why does Shane get the position."

The other boys raised their heads and blinked.

Gabe smiled. "First lesson. A scout is trustworthy. I saw

you peeking when you were told not to. Shane didn't so he's assistant patrol leader."

Kevin slouched back in his chair and folded his arms across his chest. "What do we do now?" Chuck asked.

"Now you memorize the Scout Law. Repeat after me. A boy scout is trustworthy, loyal, helpful, friendly, courteous, kind, obedient, cheerful, thrifty, brave, clean and reverent."

The Troop Master knocked on the door and leaned in. "Time to fall in, Gabe."

Has it really been an hour? "Everybody line up."

As soon as the boys were fully occupied in the game, Gabe collected his math book and stepped across the hall. The tomb quiet room contrasted sharply with the happy noise behind him. He sat at the table and opened his book. His stomach knotted and his vision began to blur as he read and re-read the problem. He ran his fingers through his hair then reached down to slam the book closed, defeated by the numbers once again.

"My son wears that look just before tossing the book across the room," she said.

He jumped. One of the new kid's moms watched him.

"Can I help?" she asked.

"I don't get math. I know I'm slow, but it doesn't make sense."

"I've been known to add a number or two. Okay if I take a look?"

Gabe made room for her on the bench. She read for a moment and then flipped the math book pages back a little and then back to the problem.

"Gabe, do you ever play video games?"

Duh, what planet did she come from? His thoughts must have shown on his face because she laughed.

"Do you ever use codes?"

"Well, yeah, it's about the only way to beat the games."

"Think of math like a video game. There're certain rules if you know them, like the codes, make it easy to win and get the right answer. This problem is trying to teach you one of those codes called the law of distribution. Here, let me show you the steps."

Gabe looked at the problem. Now it made sense.

"The answer is two, but that's easy."

"Right." She smiled like he had said something brilliant.

Gabe wrote the answer and did three more problems while she silently watched. She stood up.

"Gabe."

"Yes?"

"You did a good job with the boys tonight. They didn't know what to expect, but you made it easy and made them feel as if they belonged. A slow person couldn't have done that. The problem between you and math isn't your mind, it's how it's presented."

"Huh?"

"If you need more math help, telephone me, I'm Shane's mom and you have the number."

Gabe nodded and finished the last assigned problem. Closing the book he looked up to find himself alone in the room once again. Could she be right? Was it possible the teachers were wrong and he wasn't stupid?

More likely Daniel was right. He got lucky this time. Packing up his book, Gabe heard the yells of "fall in" and hurried back to join the closing flag ceremony.

Gabe slammed the truck door shut and snapped on his seatbelt. His father drove out of the church driveway headed home from the troop meeting. A light snow danced in front of the headlights.

"How much homework do you have left?" Dad asked.

"None, I got it all done."

"Good job. I hope you didn't have any plans for Sunday."

"Why?"

"I signed us up to help out the parents of one of the new boys."

"What're we doing?"

"They're starting up a canine search and rescue group, we're going to go out and see if we can help." His dad applied the brakes as the light changed from yellow to red. Gabe could feel the truck slip and fishtail a little.

"We don't know how to do that."

"They said they need our scouting skills for the base camp."

"What's involved with the base camp?"

"I guess we'll find out when we get there. Hey it's dogs and camping, so it has to be fun." His dad smiled and glanced his way.

"Which scout ?"

"His name is Shane."

CHAPTER 3

Gabe reached out to adjust the flow of air from the truck's heat vent into his face. His skin still burned from the chilling February wind. His dad's pick up had scratches, dents and rust spots from ten years of camping, but the heater worked just fine.

"Dad, are you sure we aren't supposed to bring a sock or something for the dogs to sniff?"

"Yup. They said just bring yourselves and plenty of patience."

"I hope they don't want us to take off a shoe once we get there; I forgot to check my socks for holes."

"I think they want the dogs alive, Gabe, so I doubt they want them sniffing teenage boys' shoes."

Laughter rolled up from Gabe's belly as he pictured some poor hound dog passed out after sniffing a sneaker.

His dad eased the truck into the school parking lot and gently applied the brakes. Even so, the truck slid a little as it came to a stop. The thaw had shifted overnight into a deep freeze. The melting snow had turned into an inch thick sheet of ice. Dad put it into park, turned off the ignition, and took his foot off the brake. The truck slid a tiny bit more then settled into place.

"Let's go, Gabe."

Heaving a sigh, Gabe climbed out. His feet slipped out from under him and he had to grab the handle to keep from landing on his butt. Heat filled his face. He glanced around waiting for people to laugh at his clumsiness. Really huge, mean-looking dogs surrounded him. They splayed their toes and used their claws to maneuver on the ice. The people with them were so focused on the dogs and their own feet that no one had noticed him.

He closed the door and did a slide shuffle along behind his dad to the entrance everyone seemed to be using. He stepped inside and froze as motionless as an ice sculpture.

Lined up in a row, watching the door intently, was german shepherd after german shepherd. No leashes, no persons next to the dogs, all of them just waiting for him to be lunch. He counted the heartbeats pounding in his ears.

The closest dog got up and trotted over to him. Gabe tensed as he waited for the pain its teeth would inflict on his body. Instead he felt a slight tickle as his fingers were given two gentle licks and then he almost fell over as the big dog wagged its tail and leaned its whole weight against him, bending his knees in the opposite direction they normally went.

"Taz, no. You were on down."

Gabe's stomach bounced off his toes as Shane hurried over and grabbed the dog's collar. The dog probably weighed twice as much as the kid. Taking it back to the spot it had left, the boy tugged on the collar. "Down. Stay". The dog instantly obeyed. Shane turned back to Gabe, gave him a sunny smile and then totally ignored the big animal at his back.

"Sorry about that, Gabe, Taz doesn't like to do the down stay command and anyone coming through the door is an excuse to break free and move. She'll be better after she gets a search or two."

"That's a she?"

"Mom says she's big for a female. I don't know, she's always been around, so she's just Taz to me."

"Is your mom a cop?"

Shane folded up with laughter. "I'm sorry, Gabe, it was the visual of my mom in a police uniform wearing a gun belt that made me laugh."

Shane grabbed Gabe's arm and pulled him over to the side so he could see around his father. Standing there was the math lady. He hadn't realized how tiny she was because he'd been sitting down. At six foot seven his dad usually towered over all people, but this woman's head was barely past his waist. It wasn't only her petiteness. Gabe figured his leg weighed more than all of her.

"That's my mom." Shane chuckled again. Gabe built the mental picture of the diminutive woman lugging a huge gun and laughed, too.

"Is your dad a policeman?" Gabe still couldn't figure out why these people would have this huge dog.

"Nah, Taz is just our pet that Mom is training for search and rescue." Shane answered.

The lady turned motioning for them to come over. Gabe hurried forward. He took the risk of patting Taz on the head as he went by and received another gentle slurp to his fingers. Shane shoved a clipboard into his hands and he followed the practice of those on the list in front of him to sign in. His dad motioned all the scouts over to the wall and calls of "Fall in" echoed up and down the line.

Mrs. O'Hara smiled at the boys. Gabe's Dad and some of the other fathers leaned against the wall behind her and watched them. They were Troop Leaders and would maintain discipline, if Gabe couldn't handle it. In Boy Scouts the boys ran things handling discipline and order as much as possible. Rank mattered. As the only Life Scout present, the second highest rank there was, the other scouts would look to him for direction.

"I want to thank all of you for coming today. What you're doing is very important work. You are actually the ones training the dogs. If you follow our directions, the dogs will learn something new," Mrs. O'Hara said.

Gabe felt perspiration gather in the small of his back. Great- here was something really important for him to mess up. He glanced down the line and saw the whispering and fidgeting increase. It looked like the others were nervous, too.

"Normally we work outside, but in weather this icy, it's too dangerous, so we were able to borrow the school for the day. You'll go hide for the dogs and play when they find you. The more animated and excited that you are, the better the dogs will like it. They won't work anymore if you're a limp fish when it comes to playing."

Murmurs went up and down the line. Gabe quickly raised two fingers in a "v" and called out "Signs up". Boy Scout speak for quiet. Silence returned as the boys quieted and raised their right hand like Gabe.

"The dogs don't need a scent article because they're taught to find any human smell, so no one take off your shirts to show off your manly form." Laughter echoed down the line until Gabe once again gave the signal for quiet.

"Okay, enough standing around talking. Let's go to work. Everybody pair up for this one." Mrs. O'Hara moved to talk to another handler as the boys broke into groups of two.

Gabe watched the others for a few moments to make sure that the process worked smoothly. Confident, then, there were no problems, he turned to the quick tug he felt at his sleeve. Shane stood next to him.

"Hey, Gabe, want to team up?" More than a little surprised that he wasn't the odd man out and having to come up with some joke about being big enough for two, Gabe nodded a yes.

"Come on, let's go for Babe." The kid had an infectious smile. With a name like Babe this should be one of the smaller sweeter dogs.

"Which one's Babe?" Gabe asked.

"See the big guy on the end, with the really dumb look?" Gabe looked down the line of dogs, they all looked huge. None of them were looking too dumb to him. The very last dog in line looked a little bigger than the rest OH, NO. Not that one.

"Yeah, that one. He loves to play tug so it's fun to be found by him." Gabe looked back to see if Shane mocked him. The kid was dead serious. Gabe sucked in his breath and tried to keep smiling.

"Let's go." Shane darted over to a pack and pulled out a red cong on a thick yellow rope. He tossed it to Gabe. "We'll need this to reward Babe when he finds us."

Babe's handler was a tall, serious man named Brian. Gabe watched as Brian asked them to keep Babe barking until he got there and directed them to a specific hallway. Shane parroted back Brian's words. Brian didn't comment or correct Shane for the repetition trick adults found so annoying.

Shane nodded his head in the direction they needed to go and they trotted down the hallway away from Brian and Babe.

"What does Brian do for a living?"

"He's a hairdresser." Shane answered.

"You're kidding!"

"Nope, Mom gets her hair done by him."

"But, he's bald."

"Yeah, and boy does he get teased about it."

Gabe shook his head. Is anyone in this place what he should be?

"Doesn't Brian get torqued when you repeat back what he tells you to do?"

"Nope. That's how we do it. It sounds silly but then the handler knows what the subject heard and the dog will be worked correctly. It's easy to miss what a handler wants and then you can mess up the whole exercise."

Shane opened the door to a classroom and pointed to the high window sill above the heaters.

"You climb up there to hide. If you don't move, the dog won't see you." He crawled into a cabinet and closed the door behind him.

The door muffled his voice. "The heat vent will probably carry your scent to Babe first. Once he barks, watch Brian for the okay. When he nods throw the toy and climb down as quick as you can, jump down if you're up to it. Babe will bring you the toy and you have to play tug until Brian says stop."

He could do this.

"Oh, and you might want to keep your hands low so you

15

don't get swatted in your privates with the toy or a nose. Babe does that a lot."

Gabe winced. "What about you?"

"After you're done, Brian will tell Babe to'find another' and he'll look for me."

Silence filled the room as they waited for the dog. Gabe's hip started to go to sleep and his neck ached from the angle that he held his head. The minutes slowly ticked away and the heated air from the vent started to make his clothes uncomfortably warm. He wasn't the right person for this job.

He wrenched his thoughts from his own discomfort to Shane in the cabinet. What if the kid ran out of air? He formed a mental picture of Shane's lifeless body flopping out of the cabinet and started running through the first aid merit badge training in his head.

"Hey, Shane, are you okay in there?"

"Yeah, this is the hard part, waiting."

Gabe heard a clicking noise outside the classroom then this weird whooshing sound like a sputtering vacuum and then Brian's voice. "What is it, Babe? Do you want to go in there?"

The doorknob rattled. The dog must've bumped it with his nose. A cool breeze washed over him as Brian opened the door. Gabe watched the dog circle the room twice. He sniffed once at Shane's cabinet then ran straight to Gabe's position and started to bark. Throwing the toy, Gabe levered himself off the shelf. By the time he landed, Babe slid into him with the toy in his mouth. His balance all a kilter, Gabe grabbed the thick yellow rope hanging out of the dog's mouth to keep from falling. A shock radiated up his arms from the tug. He could swear the dog's eyes laughed at him.

"Oh, you want to play rough, do you?" Gabe re-gripped the toy and pulled as hard as he could. The dog responded with an even sharper pull. This went on for what seemed half an hour, and Gabe couldn't stop laughing even though his breath sawed in his chest. The pure pleasure he saw in the dog's eyes was contagious. This was fun. He didn't have to hold back or be afraid of hurting anyone.

"Okay. Out, Babe." Gabe dropped the rope and then moved quickly to protect himself as Babe bumped him with the toy. Brian snatched up the cong and a few seconds later Gabe got to watch Shane muscle and tug with the big dog. Shane wore the same smile Gabe felt stretched across his own face.

"Gabe, you did a great job."

Gabe looked at Brian's face to see if he was just being polite. His arms shook. He doubted he could lift anything heavier than a soda.

"Thanks."

Brian laughed. "I mean it, most people give one or two weak tugs and let go. You did great. The dog's really fired up. He needed this."

Gabe's feet might as well have been glued to the floor as Brian and Babe left the room. He couldn't believe what he heard. Warmth ran around his insides and butterflies played in his stomach. He shook his head as he remembered Shane was still there. He turned and expected some smart remark. What he got was another big smile.

"Yes. Someone besides me to hide for Babe. That does it. You have to talk your dad into joining the team now so you can come out and hide too."

"What do you mean?" Alarms rang in his head. This was way too easy. It had to be a trick.

"Well, I was pretty sure the other guys would wimp out on Babe, but I knew you could do it. I was right. With two of us out for this dog, he'll be operational in no time."

Shane pushed Gabe toward the door. "Come on, we have to get back and see who we're going for next."

"Wait a minute, we have to do this again? My arms are like rubber."

"Yeah, it happens. All you can do is hope you get Taz or pray they take long enough finding you that your arms recover."

"Why would I want Taz?"

"When she finds you she sits in your lap and eats bits of boiled liver out of your hand." Gabe could feel his lips curling and his nose wrinkling at the thought of holding slimy liver while a ninety pound dog sat in his lap. Shane laughed.

"Now you know why I opted for Babe. By the way, push ups help build your arms so you can go for him more than once instead of having to go for Taz."

Shane jogged out of the room. Gabe followed him looking for good hiding places as he went.

"I can do this. Maybe I'll fit in with these weird people. At least I'll belong somewhere," he thought.

CHAPTER 4

"I hate Mondays," Gabe muttered, as he hunched his shoulders and shuffled to his least favorite class, math.

"If it isn't big fat Gabe, headed to math. Next semester it'll be dummy math where you belong," Daniel Case said.

Gabe felt his face flush red and saw other students in the hall turning to stare. Hunching his shoulders over more and putting his head down he scurried through the classroom door, echoes of his Daniel's laughter floated in after him. The bell rang and Mr. Lee hurried in.

"I graded Friday's tests and I have to say I am really disappointed in the entire class. I expect you to work doubly hard this week and do a lot better or I'll have to start calling your parents."

Gabe closed his eyes to block out the mental image. Hearing the rustle of papers near him, he opened his eyes and looked up to see Mr. Lee standing at his desk.

"You did much better this time Gabe, you almost made a C. It's a big improvement from your normal F. Keep trying, you might pass this course after all." Giggles escaped form the students around Gabe.

So how stupid was he? Turning over the paper, Gabe looked at the number grade "69" written on the top and circled in red. One point short of a C. Mr. Lee went over the problems on the test, and Gabe made notes as to the correct answers. Maybe Mrs. O'Hara could give him a few more math 'codes' so he would know why he got the wrong answer. That distribution trick was slick.

He walked out of class and saw Jazz. Her blond curls blocked the face of the boy whispering in her ear. The boy rested his hand on her shoulder in what looked like a caress. A pain stabbed Gab's chest. He had known that it would happen. She'd find a boyfriend. She nodded then and he saw the boy's face.

No. Not Daniel Case. How could she want to spend time with someone that mean?

Gabe turned and hurried to social studies, trying to erase the pictures his mind drew of Jazz and Daniel holding hands and kissing. Taking a seat, he pulled out his book and tried to focus on the page. Light footsteps approached and Jazz sat in the seat next to him. She had never sat this close to him before! He glanced up and she smiled at him. A furtive glance around the room told him there were plenty of empty seats further away from him. Could she really have decided to sit close to him? He risked a smile back and she nodded.

"All right class, let's begin." Mr. Harmon said. "Who can tell me the controversy associated with the bombing of Pearl Harbor?"

Gabe raised his hand. The teacher turned, smiled and pointed to him.

"There have been rumors FDR received communications that the attack was coming and he didn't do anything to prevent it or warn anyone." Gabe said.

"Good. Who can tell me why people think this?"

Jazz raised her hand. "A portion of the American population felt the oceans protected us from attack and wanted us to stay out of the war in Europe. They considered it a European problem not a world problem. By allowing the bombing to occur, the public outcry silenced those who wanted to stay out of the war."

"It's obvious some people have done their homework." Mr. Harmon turned toward the other side of the classroom and asked more questions. Jazz turned to Gabe, smiled and winked.

His stomach melted and he was glad he sat in a chair. His legs had gone so weak he didn't think he could stand up.

The bell rang and Gabe stuffed books into his backpack. He swung the pack over one shoulder and turned toward the door just as she did. He stepped back a little to make space for her to go first.

"Thanks. Hey we make a pretty good team in here, don't you think?" She said.

Gabe swallowed a lump. "Yeah. We do."

He expected her to walk away as they entered the hallway. Instead she dropped into place beside him.

"Are you going to the winter formal on Friday?" she asked.

Gabe had thought about going, but the tickets cost five weeks allowance, and he would have to rent a tuxedo. With all the ribbing he took about his clothes and his dad's job, he wasn't going to admit the problem was money. "No. Are you going?"

"I really wanted to. I mean it's one of the biggest dances of the year, but no one asked me and I'm not going alone. That would be pathetic."

Her disappointed expression made him hurt for her. "Do you want to go with me?" Had those words really come out of his mouth? Its okay, she won't want to go with someone like me.

Her face glowed. "I'd love to."

Gabe's feet stopped moving. Oh no. Now what do I do?

She had already walked two steps past him and turned back. "I have this really great red dress. Try and get a tux vest to match so the pictures look good. The dress is sleeveless so make it a wrist corsage of white flowers. I'll get you a red boutonniere." She waved and walked away.

Gabe couldn't move. He watched her go until the crowd swallowed her up. His whole body had gone cold. He couldn't tell her he couldn't afford to go, much less take a date. What had he done? Someone walking down the hallway bumped into his side. He moved his foot forward to keep from falling. He moved the other foot going in the general direction of his next class. How had he managed a date with her? Maybe things were turning around. If he could go to the winter formal with a cute date, maybe the ribbing would stop.

Gabe glanced to his right and realized he passed the school store. A sign hung in the window 'last day to get winter formal tickets'. Swallowing hard he turned and walked up to the counter. "Two tickets, please."

"That'll be fifty dollars." The clerk said.

Gabe flushed. He had about twenty dollars on him. Now what? "I don't have that much in cash."

"That's okay, I can take credit cards."

When he started high school his dad had added him to the family credit card and told him to only use it in an emergency. He hoped this qualified as an emergency. Gabe reached into his pocket and pulled out his wallet. His hand shook as he slipped the silver plastic card out of its pocket and placed it on the counter.

"Hey, do you want to add on the photographer charge now? There's a ten percent discount over paying at the door."

Jazz had talked about the pictures so he needed to buy them anyway. He might as well save the ten percent. After all a Boy Scout is thrifty. "Yeah. Add the least expensive package."

The clerk scooped up the card and dragged it through a card reader, then punched a few buttons. She tapped her fingers on the glass display in the counter until the machine spit out a small slip of paper. Without a word she passed it to him with a pen.

Gabe signed it and handed it back. The clerk passed over the tickets.

"You'll be on a list at the door for the photographer, but hang onto your receipt just in case."

Gabe tucked the tickets and receipt into his wallet and stuffed it back into his pocket and headed for class. The halls were almost empty. The bell rang. He was late. Stretching out his long legs he hurried through the closed door into the silent room.

"Gabe Turner, you of all people should not be late to this class." Miss Dole said.

"I'm sorry." Gabe slid into the first available seat.

"Everyone take out a piece of paper. Please write the symbol used on the chemical element chart as I read them off."

Gabe's hand shook as he grabbed a pen and paper. Memorization didn't work for him. He couldn't keep stuff like this in his head.

"Carbon. Oxygen. Silver. Hydrogen. Sodium. Uranium. Chlorine. Selenium. Titanium. Iron. That's it. Pass 'em in."

Gabe looked at his paper. He only had six answers written down. Even if they were all right, he'd fail this quiz.

Perfect. Just what he needed.

CHAPTER 5

Gabe walked down the three shallow steps. The heavy snow from the night before had been cleared away. His dad had been late coming home because of all the shoveling. His boots crunched salt crystals as he went.

He turned left and walked down past the line of buses. People scurried around him rushing to catch the right bus. He crossed the busy street, walked past the elementary school and started through the quiet streets of his neighborhood.

What kind of a scout was he? A scout is trustworthy. How trustworthy is it to use the family credit card when it isn't an emergency? He had to tell his dad. He hoped he wouldn't ground him.

The sound of metal sliding through snow penetrated his thoughts. He looked up and to his left. Mrs. Martin stood on her front step, shovel in hand. Her thin frame was bent with age but a smile rested on her lips. She wore a hand knit stocking cap, a bulky wool coat and high heeled boots.

"Mrs. Martin. You shouldn't be shoveling." Gabe hurried through the knee deep wet snow. He dropped his pack on the tiny cleared spot and took the shovel from her hands. "I'll do it."

"Oh thank you Gabe. The man who usually shovels called me. This snow has him busy as a one-armed paper hanger and he said he couldn't come until the end of the week." She pulled off her hat and ran her fingers through her short grey curls. "I told him I'd take care of it, but this stuff is a lot heavier than I thought."

Gabe cleared the steps while she watched.

"You do a nice job. Nicer than he does. You even dig around my flower urns."

"No problem."

Gabe had gotten into a rhythm. Swing in, lift, twist, toss, step. He was halfway down the walk when she re-appeared with a black leather purse in her hand. He stopped and leaned on the shovel. He could feel sweat running down his face.

She hung her purse on her arm and put out her hand with several folded bills. "Here you go, fifteen dollars. That's what I pay the other fellow."

Gabe stared at the money. "I can't take it. We're neighbors."

"Oh posh. I would've paid it and I'd rather pay a neighbor than someone who leaves me buried for days at a time." She tucked the folded money into his gloved hand.

He made a fist around it and closed his eyes. Maybe I can pay Dad back. When he opened his eyes she was staring at him intently.

"What's wrong Gabe?"

"Nothing. This is a big help, that's all." He was glad his face was flushed from shoveling.

"Are your folks having money troubles, honey?" a gentle hand reached up to rest on his shoulder. Concern showed in every feature of her face. He didn't want her thinking that about his parents.

"No. I goofed up and spent money today I shouldn't have."

She scanned his face closely, and then nodded. "You know Mrs. Taglia and the Petersons use the same man I do. How's about I call and see if they want you to shovel them out, too?"

Forty-five dollars wasn't all of it but it would help. He smiled and nodded.

She disappeared inside and returned as he finished the walk.

"They'd love to have you dig them out."

"Thank you. Do you mind if I borrow your shovel?"

"Go for it."

*****

An hour later Gabe met his father on the side walk in front of their house. His dad's expression changed to one of relief. "Gabriel, where have you been? I was getting worried."

"I'm sorry Dad. I was shoveling snow for some of the neighbors."

His dad turned back toward the house and put an arm around his shoulders. "I'm glad you were able to help out."

Gabe dug the cash out of his pocket and held it out toward his Dad. "Here's what they paid me."

"You earned it you keep it." His dad opened the front door and waved Gabe in before him.

Gabe stepped inside, dropped his backpack by the door and dropped the money on the table.

"No, Dad, it's your money." He took a deep breath. "I used the credit card and I shouldn't have. I owe you more than this, but if it snows some more I can earn the rest to pay you back."

Dad stood there staring at him and then the money. The silence stretched out and Gabe felt his stomach knotting.

"What did you buy and how much was it?"

"Two tickets to the winter formal and the photo package. It was eighty dollars all together."

"Two tickets? Who's the other one for?"

"A girl I asked to go with me."

"How long have you been planning this?"

"I wasn't. It just happened."

Dad inhaled deeply then sighed. "If it's a formal then there are going to be more costs to rent a tuxedo, aren't there?"

Gabe swallowed and nodded. His voice had stopped working.

"If I recall the signs, the dance is Friday."

Gabe nodded again.

Dad pulled his keys out of his pocket. "Get in the truck."

"Why?" That doesn't sound like my voice.

"We need to get to the formal store before they close."

Gabe scrambled for the door. He had it halfway open and

stopped to turn back to his Dad. "Thanks for not being mad."

"I'm not mad, just disappointed. But then when I think about how hard it was to ask a girl for a date when I was your age, I can see how this could happen."

Gabe turned back to the door.

"Gabriel."

"Yes."

"Next time try and plan it."

CHAPTER 6

Gabe stepped from the frigid temperatures outside into the entry of his house and stopped. The warm humid air condensed on his cold glasses and blurred his vision. He closed the door, unzipped his coat, and cleaned the fog from the lenses with the tail of his plaid flannel shirt.

"Gabe?" His dad stuck his head out of the kitchen, one of his mom's pink frilly aprons on over his Boy Scout uniform. "Mom called. She was able to order the corsage from Debbie's Florist. I'll pick it up for you Friday morning when I pick up the tux."

"Thanks." This was unbelievable, he thought. He was so glad that he had his parents.

"Hurry up and get your homework done. We have scouts tonight."

Gabe went to his room, changed into his uniform shirt and sat at his desk. He only had a couple of math problems left, which gave him time to daydream.

Today had been perfect. Jazz had sat next to him in English and social studies. They'd shared smiles and winks. Life was good. Maybe when he made Eagle, she'd come and meet his family.

"Supper's ready."

It sounded like his dad had shouted from the kitchen. He could hear his mom's voice. It was a standing joke that Dad shouted and Mom asked him if he'd been raised in a barn.

Gabe closed his book and hurried into dinner. The aroma made his mouth water. He tucked a big napkin into the front of his shirt as he scrambled into his chair. Mom came in with hot garlic bread and Dad carried the lasagna. Once they sat down Gabe reached for a slab of the entrée while Mom scooped salad on her plate and Dad took a hunk of bread from the basket.

Gabe forked the steaming pasta into his mouth and savored the melting cheese. It seemed like only a few bites and his first piece disappeared. He reached for a second helping. "Mom thanks for ordering the flowers."

She smiled at him. "I was glad to help. I was so worried with the short notice no one would take the order, but Debbie's Florist were great about it."

She paused to eat a bite of salad. "From now on they're going to get all my flower orders."

He reached for a third helping.

"Gabe, we gotta go. You can have thirds when we get home." Dad said.

Gabe settled the spatula back into the lasagna pan. He picked up his plate and glass, rinsed them and loaded them into the dishwasher. "I'll get my neckerchief and meet you at the truck." He caught his parents kiss good bye as he hurried from the kitchen to his room.

Wonder if I'll be able to kiss Jazz? he thought.

*****

They were early so he leaned against the wall next to his dad and watched the new patrol.

Chuck took his new rank seriously. "Everyone line up. I'm first, then Shane, then Kevin. Keep even spacing. Stand up straight. Joe, tuck in your shirt. Peter why don't you have your patch sewn on your uniform?"

Oh not good. Chuck's going way overboard. Gabe turned slightly and tapped the Troop Master's arm. "Mr. C, should I stop this?"

Mr. Carter turned to watch Chuck's imitation of a drill sergeant and turned back to Gabe. "No. Take him aside when we break into small groups. If you do it now, you'll embarrass him in front of the whole patrol. This is part of learning how to be a good leader. Some push too hard, some don't push hard enough. Give him a quiet talk and see if that fixes things."

Gabe nodded and turned back to observe. He noticed that sunny Shane had lost his smile and his eyes were changing color, as the sky in a storm. Gabe had thought they were blue, but as he watched they shifted to grey and then green.

"Chuck, I need to talk to Gabe." Shane said and walked away before Chuck could answer.

The kid seemed to be taking big deep breaths, holding them and then letting them out. Gabe lowered his voice so it wouldn't carry beyond Shane. "Are you okay? Do you have asthma or something?"

Shane closed his eyes and was silent for a few seconds. When he opened them he smiled, it looked forced, but he smiled. "No, I'm okay. Chuck was just getting under my skin and I needed to walk away. Can we pretend to be talking about the search team before I do something unchristian?"

Gabe smiled and nodded. Unchristian, where does he come from? The kid's eyes were turning blue again; the storm had passed.

"Do your eyes change color?" Gabe asked.

"Probably. When my dad gets really angry his eyes go from blue to grey to green. If they were doing that then I inherited it from him. I almost lost my temper with Chuck. That's why I came over here," Shane said.

"Good to know. I think I may start calling you the green-eyed monster."

Shane made a face and rolled his eyes.

Mr. Carter turned back to Gabe and his Dad. "Rich, Gabe, I was looking through your Eagle packet and you didn't list a church. You're going to need a recommendation from a member of the clergy, along with teachers and unrelated adults."

"Don, I haven't seen the inside of a church in twelve years except to come here for Scout meetings. If I showed up for services the roof would probably cave in." Dad answered.

"Well that might give a bunch of Scouts the service hours they need to fix it." Mr. Carter said. Gabe liked the slow gentle pace of Mr. Carter's voice. He never seemed to talk fast or get angry but he always got people to do what needed to be done.

"You need to look at going to a church, any church, or a synagogue, or a temple, any house of worship. Remember a Scout is reverent. With all the flack the organization has been taking to remove the requirements to worship God, the review committee is going to be looking for that recommendation. The ACLU has been on a big campaign to get the Boy Scouts to allow atheists to join. They've been lodging complaints to force Scout troops out of meeting in public buildings and schools. If we want to believe in God, we apparently have to keep it on church property. It's becoming a real problem so national is going to be sensitive to it."

"I don't want to prevent Gabe from getting his Eagle. He's worked too hard to get this far for me to let him down." Dad's face wore a grim expression. Gabe had never seen his dad so serious. What was going on? Gabe thought that they never went to church because there was always too much to do.

Shane stepped forward and lightly tugged on the Troop Master's sleeve. "Mr. Carter? If the Turners don't want to go to church, Gabe could come with us. Our minister'll understand. Besides, if Gabe comes without his parents it will give Reverend Allen something special to write about in the recommendation."

Mr. Carter looked from Shane to Dad. "How about it Rich? Can Gabe go with the O'Hara family?"

Gabe held his breath and waited. Finally his dad sighed and shifted his position against the wall.

"It sounds like a solution that'll work. I really don't want to go to church, Don." Dad said.

"Good. I'll talk to Jim O'Hara about Shane's offer. I don't think it'll be a problem," Mr. Carter said and walked away.

His dad pushed away from the wall and refused to meet Gabe's eyes. "If you need me, I'll be outside checking the camping gear."

What was wrong? Why did this upset Dad? Gabe watched his father leave the room without a backward glance. Looking down, he saw Shane watching him.

"Thanks, Shane. My Eagle rank almost became mission impossible for a minute there."

Shane smiled a real smile this time. "No problem. That's what friends are for."

Shouts of "fall in" echoed around the room. Shane hurried back to his place in line and Gabe took his position behind the patrol and saluted as the color guard marched up front with the American and Troop flags. The word 'friend' bounced around inside his head.

"How did I manage a date and a friend all in one week? I wonder if I can manage a decent first kiss, too?" Gabe said to himself.

CHAPTER 7

Gabe pulled the red bow tie into place and reached behind his neck to fasten the snaps. He had finally gotten the tightness adjusted right and reached up to twist the bow straight. He took the black jacket from the hanger and slipped it on.

His brown curly hair was freshly washed and he'd even used some gel to hold it in place. Someday he'd have enough face hair to need to shave. For now he was safe from razor nicks.

The shine on his rented dress shoes reflected the white of his shirt. One last look in the mirror and he headed to the living room for his mom's inspection.

"Oh Gabe, you look all grown up and so handsome." Mom said. "Rich, get a picture."

His dad snapped pictures until Gabe turned away. It was that or get red in the face. Dad took the hint and put the camera back in its case.

"Get your coat." Gabe slipped on his coat and walked out to the truck. For the first time he really noticed the rust spots and dents. He was glad Jazz wanted to meet at the school instead of Dad picking her up. She probably wouldn't want to be seen showing up in a beat up old pick up. It almost made Gabe want to walk to the dance, but that would surely wreck the shine on his shoes.

Gabe's dad got in and slammed his door. The engine roared

to life and they backed out onto the street. It took less than five minutes to pull up in front of the school.

"Have you got your phone?" Dad asked.

Gabe patted his pockets until he felt the familiar lump. "Yup."

"Call me when the dance ends and I'll come get you. Make sure your date knows I can drive her home."

"Okay." Gabe got out and slammed the door with his left hand. His right held the clear plastic box with the white rosebud and red ribbon corsage. He watched his dad drive out of the school before turning toward the doors. Most of the school was dark. The main entrance had two bright search lights shooting columns of light into the sky. Inside was dimmer but flashes occurred at regular intervals as the photographer snapped arrival pictures. Gabe felt for his wallet to make sure he had the receipt and walked up the steps.

He couldn't believe he was actually on a real date with her. He couldn't believe he spent over a hundred dollars, but she was worth it. With her hair up, she'll looked like a fairy princess, Gabe thought.

He walked in and glanced around the room, looking for Jazz and her red dress.

Nothing. Then, laughter off to his left drew his attention.

Jazz stood there a vision in sapphire blue, with her blonde hair swept up and piled on top of her head. She laughed so hard that she had to lean on Daniel Case's arm. His vest perfectly matched Jazz's dress. In his turn, his laughter was so deep that it made tears roll down his cheeks.

"Oh Turner, if you could see your face right now!" Daniel's voice trailed off into more laughter.

Gabe said, "I don't understand, Jazz. You said you were wearing red. I got the vest to match just like you wanted." He didn't want to believe she would do this to him.

Daniel bent at the waist laughing so hard. Jazz joined him.

"Oh Gabe, you really didn't believe I could be interested in someone like you? It was a joke. Can't you see how funny this is?" she answered.

After laughing some more she continued, "I thought you'd figure it out when I said I was wearing red. No one in his right mind would wear that color." She glanced at his bright vest and started to giggle, "Except you."

Daniel chimed in. "You said 'in his right mind', but this is dummy Gabe. It answers your question." The two of them went off in gales of laughter once more. Other people were starting to stare.

Gabe looked down at the plastic box in his hand. With a flick of his wrist, he flung it at her feet. "No Jazz, I don't think it's funny and if you weren't as shallow as a dry creek you'd know just what a cruel trick you pulled."

Gabe turned toward the door, and then stopped to look back. "You may be pretty on the outside but you've got to be the ugliest person I've every met."

"How dare you—"

The door closed, shutting off the remainder of her response. Gabe turned down the sidewalk and started for home. He couldn't hold the tears back, but it didn't matter, for no one was on the deserted streets to see his humiliation.

He had the tears under control by the time he got home. He opened the front door and slammed it shut. Both his parents rushed from the living room.

"Gabe, what happened?" His Mom asked.

"It was a joke. A big fat joke on big fat stupid Gabe. I'm never asking a girl out again."

He turned on his heel and ran to his room slamming the door behind him. He removed the tie and tux with sharp jerky motions, tossing the garments in a pile in the general direction of the hanger. He pulled on sweats, turned out the lights and climbed into bed without brushing his teeth.

He didn't care if they rot out of his head. Nobody's ever going to like me anyway.

He heard a soft knock and then his dad step quietly in. "Gabe?"

"What?"

"I'm so sorry this happened. I didn't think people could be that cruel. Do you want to talk?"

"No. I want to go to sleep and never wake up." Tears started to choke his voice.

He heard his dad feeling his way across the room in the darkness. The bed sagged as he sat beside Gabe and rubbed his back. "You know the best revenge on someone who does something this mean?"

"No." The pillow muffled his voice and hopefully hid the tears.

"Doing something spectacular and proving how wrong they were."

Gabe rolled onto his side to look at his Dad's face, not caring if he saw the tears. "That's the problem, I'm not capable of anything spectacular."

"Yes you are."

"What? I can't even pass dummy math."

"You can be an Eagle."

Gabe wiped his eyes on his sleeve. "That's not spectacular."

"Really? Then why do only four scouts out of a hundred make it to Eagle?" His dad stood up and collected the hanger, bag and discarded clothes from the floor. Just before he closed the door, he turned back toward Gabe.

"Think about it. They don't win until you give up." The door closed quietly behind him.

Gabe rolled one way only to flip over to another. Every time he closed his eyes he heard her laughter. His stomach churned and grumbled. The house was quiet, too quiet. More noise came from his stomach. Heaving a sigh he threw back the covers and padded bare foot into the kitchen. Two glasses of milk and a bag of Oreos later, he crawled back into bed. He had spent the whole school year going to sleep with a vision of her in his mind, and it was hard to drift off without it. He closed his eyes but saw Jazz and Daniel laughing. Nope. Wrong picture.

Then he started to imagine his Eagle court of honor and telling her she wasn't welcome.

CHAPTER 8

Gabe reached in his closet and pulled out a pair of khaki pants and a light blue, button-down shirt. Shane had called yesterday and left a message saying that he shouldn't dress up for church. The message didn't make sense; it was something about the minister not caring if he showed up wearing a barrel and a pair of Mickey Mouse ears as long as he came. Gabe should have taken the call instead of hiding in his room but his nerves were too raw from the dance the night before. With the way his luck had been running, that probably had cost him his only friend. Gabe decided not to take any chances. If his becoming an Eagle Scout rested on this pastor's recommendation, then he intended to make a good impression. He knew if he got his Eagle people would have to give him some respect.

Clean and dressed, he took a deep breath and walked out of his room toward the kitchen. The sun had barely risen and shadows shrouded the rooms. The quiet told him his parents slept. A slow, gentle snow fell outside the windows and piled in soft drifts against the fence.

He decided to make oatmeal, not the instant stuff where the oats got stuck in his teeth, but real, creamy cooked oatmeal. He'd made it a bunch of times over an open fire so using the stove was a snap.

He watched the oats and water boil and blend into a smooth paste. He constantly stirred the mixture in slow easy strokes.

When bubbles slowly popped and left a hole for a second, he pulled the pan off the heat and dumped the contents into a bowl. He heaped three big spoonfuls of brown sugar on top. He had his head buried in the refrigerator looking for the cream when a man's shadow caught his eye. He jumped back until he recognized his dad, his face buried in the shadows, leaning on the doorframe wearing pajama bottoms, a white tee shirt and bare feet.

"Dad, you scared me to death." Gabe walked to the table and poured the thick cream in a circle on top of the sugar. Lines of the brown sweetener floated to the surface. Dad walked over and sat down at the table and fiddled with the cream carton while Gabe spooned the sweet concoction into his mouth.

"There's five dollars on the hall table," Dad said. "At some point, they'll pass a collection plate and you'll be expected to put something in."

Gabe looked up and nodded, his mouth too full to answer.

"Gabe, I want you to take what's said in church with a grain of salt. Preachers have a way of making you believe there really is a God out there who cares and will help you. I don't want you to depend on Him and be let down. Depend on yourself and what you can do, no one else."

"Don't you believe in God?"

He shrugged, "I want to protect you from the hurt and disappointment I've felt. Believing there is some Omnipotent Being who cares about you will only get you hurt. I wanted you in Scouts so you could learn to be self-reliant."

Gabe watched his dad stand, then slowly leave the room.

Gabe finished his breakfast in silence and watched the snow fall. His Dad's words kept replaying in his mind. Dad doesn't believe but the O'Hara's and Mr. C do. Who's right?

He rinsed his dishes and tiptoed to his room to grab his wallet and house key. He pocketed the bill his dad had left him and grabbed his jacket from the closet. Less than five minutes later the O'Hara SUV pulled up. He slipped out quietly and ran to the door Shane held open for him.

CHAPTER 9

Mr. O'Hara parked in front of the yellow brick building. Even though twice the number of cars decorated the parking lot as there were for a troop meeting, he'd been hoping for more people to hide his mistakes.

"Not many people here today, huh." Gabe tried to be nonchalant but his palms started to sweat.

"I dunno. I guess there's about a hundred people that come to each of the services."

"There's more than one service?"

Shane nodded.

"Do we have to stay for all of them?"

"No way. Only the minister and the choir have to do that. We go to early service so afterwards we can go to brunch."

Gabe sighed. "Can your parents drop me off at home before you go eat? I didn't bring any money except for the collection plate."

"Do you want to go home? I mean if you do, it's all right, it would be nice to have a friend along instead of being stuck with my parents."

Mrs. O'Hara had walked up behind Shane as he talked.

"Visitors aren't expected to contribute to the church, Gabe." She smiled at him. "We planned on taking you to brunch with us, our treat. That way we don't have to entertain Shane." She winked.

"Mom." Shane rolled his eyes and made a face.

Gabe laughed, his first since Friday's disaster. "I'll see if it's okay."

They walked up four shallow steps and entered through two big white doors. A smiling, heavy set, blonde lady in black slacks and sweater walked to them ready to shake hands. "Good morning and welcome."

Gabe wondered if she was the minister.

"Good morning, Doreen. How are the kids?" Mrs. O'Hara asked.

"Fine. They're getting excited about the summer mission trip," their greeter answered. Doreen turned to shake Shane's and Gabe's and Mr. O'Hara's hands. Her "good morning" and firm handshake were as cheerful and friendly to Gabe as to the O'Hara's. She looked him square in the eye and smiled.

Wow, she's nice and she doesn't even know me. Please don't let me trip or something, Gabe pleaded silently to a Higher Authority.

As they moved forward, Gabe could see a fire burned in the fireplace. It made the room comfortable, almost like a living room. The wood floor looked old, but shone. The white walls had some decorative trim, but overall it didn't seem like a ritzy place. Some of the tension left his muscles.

He thought to himself, ' I'll have to ask Shane what a mission trip is. Wish I could just sit in front of the fire and listen.'

A balding older man smiled and handed each of them a bulletin and they followed Mrs. O'Hara up the aisle.

"Hey, Mom, let's sit here." Shane had stopped at a pew several rows back from where Mrs. O'Hara stood. He turned to Gabe and whispered, "If you don't watch her she plunks us in the first row. We don't sing well enough to sit up there."

"Sing?" Gabe felt his voice break on the end of the word. "My singing sounds like a croaking frog."

Mrs. O'Hara slipped into the pew first and turned to him. "Don't worry Gabe, the Bible says make a joyful noise, not carry a tune. You'll do fine. Try not to lip-synch like Shane."

Shane and Mrs. O'Hara pulled out the black hymnals stored in a rack under the pew in front of them.

"Open the bulletin," Mrs. O'Hara said.

He opened the booklet and read off the song numbers to her. She marked each one with a ribbon attached to the hymnal. Gabe glanced through the pages. It seemed pretty straight forward and clear, all he had to do was follow along. "Mrs. O'Hara, how do I know when to kneel and when to stand up?"

"See the asterisks on the right side? Stand when you see them, otherwise sit down. No kneeling."

"That's a relief, I can't mess this up. If the minister figures out what a klutz I am he may not give me my recommendation", Gabe said to himself.

The organist played a classical piece. After a few seconds of silence, the church bells rang. Everyone quieted and a slender young man in a coarse weave, white robe walked up the aisle. He knelt in front of the cross and obviously said a prayer then walked to the pulpit.

"Good morning. Welcome to Community Church. I'm Reverend Allen Walters. We have a lot going on in our community and I'd like to call your attention to the announcements in the bulletin."

Instead of hearing the minister, Gabe heard the standard troop response to the word 'announcements' in his head. It was a silly song all the boys sang in unison. He shook his head to clear it.

"If you're comfortably able, please stand and join us in hymn number twelve, I Sing the Mighty Power of God."

Mrs. O'Hara opened the hymnal while the organist played through the chorus. Both she and Mr. O'Hara started to sing. Shane's lips were moving but no sound came out. Taking the cue, Gabe started mouthing the words until he got an elbow in the ribs and the "you're messing up" look from Mrs. O'Hara. A kind of croaking sound came out of his throat and finally turned into words.

Shane gave him a weird look and kept lip-syncing.

Oh no, buddy. If I get the elbow you do, too. Gabe jabbed his own elbow into Shane's side. A squeak and then the words to the song rewarded his efforts.

Once the choir came by, filling the room with music, carrying the tune became easier. After the song, Reverend Walters led a responsive prayer. The words were printed on the page.

"All right, I haven't messed up so far," Gabe reassured himself softly.

"Let us pass the peace," Reverend Walters said.

Now what?

The whole congregation milled around exchanging greetings. Even the minister had walked halfway down the aisle, shaking hands and greeting people. Suddenly the organist started playing. It sounded like she had really cranked the thing up to get everyone's attention.

Reverend Walters sprinted back to the pulpit.

"Glory be to the Father..." The O'Haras and most of the people were singing, while hurrying back to their seats. No one looked at a hymnal. Gabe flipped open the bulletin and found the words and music. He joined in just before they got to the "Amen".

A man as tall as Gabe's dad, but about half his weight, stood and walked quickly to the front of the sanctuary to a stand holding a big Bible and a microphone.

"Our first reading is from Romans, chapter eight, verses thirty-one through thirty nine. 'Who dares accuse us whom God has chosen for his own? No one—for God himself has given us right standing with himself. Who then will condemn us? No one—for Christ Jesus died for us and was raised to life for us, and He is sitting in the place of honor at God's right hand, pleading for us'."

Gabe shifted in his seat and leaned forward a little. Is condemn anything like putting people down? It would be really nice if he had someone who'd stop everyone from doing that to him.

"What would it be like to have someone plead for me?" Gabe asked himself.

The man who had been reading returned to his seat. Reverend Walters moved to the pulpit. The first words out of his mouth were,

"Who loves ya, baby?"

Huh? Gabe was startled.

Reverend Walters continued. "Think about it for a second. No matter what you do, no matter what happens to you. You can count on God loving you. When it comes down to it, God's love is the only constant."

Gabe leaned back again and tuned the minister out, thinking,

"So even though no one at school likes me and I don't fit in, God still loves me? There's got to be a catch. Why would He love me? I don't pray or go to church, I'm not important. I'm clumsy and can't learn like everyone else. Why would He love me? Nobody else even likes me."

A baby started crying several pews behind him. Since everyone else ignored the noise He didn't turn to look, even though he wanted to. He focused on listening again.

"We have all heard Jesus' parable of the lost sheep. He begins the parable with a question – 'Which of you, having a hundred sheep and losing one of them, does not leave the ninety-nine in the wilderness and go after the one that is lost until he finds it?' Economic common sense says cut your losses and yet Jesus makes this sound like a no-brainer. Why?"

Gabe looked out the window. The snow continued to fall.

"If this keeps up, I'll be able to shovel walks again and pay my parents back some more. But where is this guy going with this?" he thought impatiently.

"But if you've been the one who has walked that sheep to the pasture day in and day out for years, you've got more than just an economic investment, your emotions are involved. Isn't emotional investment a way of describing love?"

"Okay, now I get it. It was like when I lost my hat. It was a ratty old thing and I had three more, better ones at home. But it was special, it was my camp out hat and I spent almost an hour searching until I found it," Gabe said to himself.

"Love goes to extremes when common sense says 'enough already'. Love is placing a higher value on something or someone than the market will bear."

"So Jesus says a lost sheep is special. Great. So what's that got to do with the other reading?" Gabe asked himself

"We all know Jesus as the Good Shepherd and we're His flock, but who were the sinners? Sinners were seen as little better than rats. Today they'd probably be telemarketers. They weren't someone you invited to dinner. As a matter of fact, if they sat next to a Pharisee, the Pharisee would have been insulted, stood up and made a huge embarrassing scene. To most they were a worthless waste of time, expendable. But Jesus welcomed them. Jesus loved them, no matter what."

"I don't know what a Pharisee is but sounds like Daniel and Jazz acted like them and treated me like a sinner. So does that mean Jesus would invite me over for dinner?" Gabe stifled a laugh at the silly image of himself sitting down to dinner with Jesus and the disciples like in that famous painting, they in their long robes and himself in jeans and a tee-shirt.

"It's no wonder that people Jesus interacted with knew the depth of His love, a love so deep it transcended human limitations. This love had to be from God. Jesus shows us that we are precious in God's sight, each and every one of us. Though it may defy common sense or even our own sense of self worth, Christ shows us that God loves us and is willing to do whatever it costs to save sinners, like you and me. That's who Jesus lived to save, that's who Jesus died to save. That's not common sense, that's pure love. Amen."

Silence filled the room for a few seconds then the soft noises of fabric rubbing against fabric, books being opened, pages turned and people standing.

"Wait, so Jesus loves me as I am and He died to save me? Save me from what?" Gabe thought as he looked down at the bulletin. Printed on the cover was, 'That everyone who believes may have everlasting life' John 3:16.

'With the way things have been going why would I want

life to go on forever? Life is the pits. Would it be different if I believed?" he wondered.

"Let us pray."

Gabe saw everyone else bow their head and quickly copied them.

Reverend Walters said, "Thank you, gracious God, for making your home with us and claiming us as your own people. We dedicate ourselves and our gifts toward the new world you are building among us – a world where peace emerges from mutual respect, honest encounters, and Christ's love shared among neighbors. May that love be reflected in our attitudes and actions when we are together and when we are apart. Amen." Reverend Walters said, "Our closing hymn is number one, 'Immortal, Invisible, God Only Wise'."

Jesus died to make a better world where people respect each other. Is that why so many people believe? But why doesn't Dad believe then?

Gabe sang the words without really seeing the print nor the music. His body shivered, but he really wasn't cold. Could it be possible for God to change him into something of value? Who could he talk to? Not Dad. Maybe Mrs. O'Hara, but what would she think of his stupid questions and she'd tell his dad about the problems in school. But then whom? Whom could he trust?

Shane might hold the answers.

CHAPTER 10

Gabe popped open the top of the can of pineapple and drained the juice into two paper cups. The white tent overhead flapped and snapped like thunder in the wind. He and his dad had prepared lunch for the team on a table that stood against the side of the big white base camp truck. The vehicle protected them from the worst of the icy blast.

"Will I go hide with Shane again? If not, when do I ask him about this God thing? How do I ask him?" Gabe wondered.

When he couldn't get any more juice out, by shaking the can, he turned it upright and finished removing the top.

"Who's the second cup for?" Dad asked.

"Shane," Gabe answered. "Mrs. O'Hara gave us the choice of cleaning up after the carsick puppy or helping with KP. He volunteered for the clean-up job so I figure he deserves half." Gabe watched his dad stir the onions, peppers and sausage in the frying pan.

"Okay God, not sure if you're listening, but if you are, help me through this one. I don't know what to do."

He turned back to the dump cake he was making. A quick flick of his wrist and pineapple pieces smacked the cake tin. He shook the pan to spread them around and then added canned cherry pie filling over the top. It didn't take long to sprinkle the yellow cake mix over the fruit and add the can of Seven-Up.

He lifted the dessert into a dutch oven and buried the whole thing in the coals in the barbeque grill.

"Hey Gabe, got anything for breakfast over here?" Shane walked up and washed his hands in a basin of hot water.

"Doughnuts, hot chocolate and pineapple juice."

"Let me at 'em." Shane dried his hands on a towel hanging from one of the tent support posts.

"Better do the juice first." Gabe handed him one of the paper cups and downed the other.

Shane gulped his juice and moved to the grill, extending his hands toward the warmth. Gabe's dad poured hot chocolate into cups and handed them to Shane and Gabe.

"What else do we need to do, Dad?"

"You're done until they need victims to hide for the dogs."

"Subjects." Shane said.

"What?"

"The dogs look for subjects. The difference between a subject and a victim is whether we look for them or not." Shane grinned from ear to ear. "It's a joke we sometimes play on newbies."

"Aren't we newbies?" Gabe asked.

"Naw, you're keepers."

Gabe felt warmth radiate from his stomach and it had nothing to do with the hot sweet drink. Here was a place that people wanted him.

"Will they still want me if I ask Shane a lot of stupid questions? Maybe I should keep my questions to myself," he wondered.

Mr. O'Hara walked into the tent and poured himself a cup of chocolate. "Gabe, have you earned the orienteering merit badge?"

"No sir." So much for being a keeper.

"Not a problem. I just needed to know your skill level. By the time we're through you should be able to apply for the badge." He took a sip of his drink. "We'll send you out with Shane this time and next training we'll start on pace count and heading information so you can go alone and we can work two dogs at the same time."

Gabe felt the heat of a blush warm his face. He had to have an eleven year old kid take care of him. Would there ever be a time he could take care of himself? He'd grab the merit badge booklet on orienteering at the next troop meeting and find a way to learn it even if it killed him.

"Grab your gear and do a refill on the chocolate and then we'll get you out for the dogs."

Gabe put his drink on the table next to Shane's, snapped a lid on it and then hurried out of the tent after his friend.

"Shane, what are we going to be doing?"

"Pretty much the same as in the school. Sit still and wait for the dogs to find us then play like crazy. Only thing is, the dogs'll work a bigger area than at the school, so it'll take a lot longer to be found."

"Is it okay to cover up with a blanket while we wait?"

"Tarp, blanket and sleeping bag, if you want. Take what you need to stay warm. We can even rig a windbreak shelter."

Gabe nodded and turned to his Dad's truck. They'd stuffed camping gear into every nook and cranny. He'd learned how to stay warm in cold weather a long time ago. He stuffed a tarp and sleeping bag into an old pack along with socks, heavy gloves and a scarf and slipped it on his back. He closed the cap window and trotted back to the tent.

Shane followed him. The kid's pack looked like it would tip him over backwards. Gabe turned to the table and topped off the drinks they'd left behind to hide his smile at the funny picture Shane made.

Mr. O'Hara spread out a topographical map on the table and waved them over.

"Base camp is here." Mr. O'Hara pointed with a pencil. "We need you to be here, just over the hill." He drew a straight line between the two points.

The curved brown lines stacked inside one another reminded Gabe of the shape of the hill behind the truck. He realized where the hill is, but did not know how to find the exact spot where Mr. O' Hara was pointing.

Shane pulled out his compass and lined up the base plate with the vertical lines on the map, then slid it over until the center of the compass was on the base camp end of the line.

"So we need to go off at a heading of ninety-eight degrees, right?" Shane asked.

Mr. O'Hara looked over his son's shoulder. "Yup. Can you figure the distance?"

"Easy. Three thousand feet."

How did he figure that?

"Load up on snacks, give me a radio check and hit the road. We're burning daylight." Mr. O'Hara smiled at them and waved toward the table of doughnuts.

Shane grabbed two vanilla long johns, stuffed one in his mouth, and he wrapped the other in plastic and put it in his pocket. He snatched up the radio and started talking with his mouth full. "Subject one radio check."

"Subject one from base, next time try it without the dough-nut in your mouth." Mr. O'Hara answered into the base radio.

Shane looked at Gabe and nodded toward the tent flap. Gabe followed him outside but he stopped about ten feet from the truck and pulled out his compass.

"What's up? Did you forget something?" Gabe asked.

"If I take the headings any closer to base than this, all the metal throws my compass off."

Gabe watched as the red needle slowly stopped swing-ing and Shane lined it up with the red box on the dial then he turned his whole body until the arrow pointed to the hash mark for ninety-eight degrees. He looked straight up from the needle and then turned and looked back over his shoulder. He closed the compass with a snap and started off in the direction the ar-row had been pointing.

"I get it. That's how we know which direction to go. But how do we know when we've gone far enough?" He glanced over at Shane and realized he was counting.

"What're you doing?"

"Counting paces. Every two steps is a pace and my pace is around five feet. We need to go three thousand feet so that's six hundred paces."

Gabe froze in place. Could it be this easy? Shane had stopped for a big bramble patch.

"Now what?"

"We circle around the patch." He did a sharp ninety degree turn and started walking along the side of the patch. When he was passed it, he did another turn back in the direction he'd been going. As soon as they got by the obstacle he headed for their original line.

"See that tree with the branch hanging way up?" Shane asked.

"Yeah."

"Now see the base camp truck?"

"Yeah."

"When the truck is directly behind us and the tree is directly in front we're back on our original line of travel." Shane smiled and took off toward the tree.

Gabe shook his head and hurried after the younger boy. Would everything the kid had to teach him be this easy? Shane sure didn't act like Gabe was some dummy for not knowing. Could he ask the questions the sermon had raised in his mind or would he be better off keeping his mouth shut?

Shane stopped suddenly. "This is it."

They were in the middle of an open field at the bottom of two hills. The hills channeled the air through their spot like a wind tunnel. One look at Shane's face told Gabe he wasn't happy. "What's wrong?"

"We're going to freeze out here. I think I need to radio in and see if we can change locations even though it'll change the problem they wanted to work with the dogs. There're no trees to anchor the tarps to." Shane reached for his radio.

"Wait. We can anchor the tarps with the packs and dig in the edge. We'll be fine." Gabe pulled a trenching tool from his pack. Shane nodded and pulled a tarp out of his gear. Gabe cut the trench in the snow and Shane came behind shoving the edges of his and Gab's tarps into the slot and pressing the icy crystals firmly down on top. A few minutes later and they tucked themselves into sleeping bags sandwiched between the two tarps, the down wind corners held in place by the weight of their packs.

Shane pulled his radio out of his coat. "Base from subjects. We're in place."

"Ten-four. Subjects are in place. Unit three is commencing sector."

Shane let go of the radio and fished the long john and spill-proof cup of hot chocolate out of his pocket. The food looked unappetizing in the strange blue light filtering in through the tarp

"So, what'd you think of our church?"

CHAPTER 11

Gabe shoved his own doughnut into his mouth to buy a second to think. It was decision time. He could ask questions or he could shut up.

"I liked it." Good. That shouldn't upset anyone.

"Yeah. The people are nice and Reverend Walters is young enough to be cool. Chuck says he has trouble staying awake at his church during the sermon. Even though Mom gets us up at the crack of dawn to go, I can stay awake without a problem with Pastor Allen."

Gabe gathered his breath. Maybe he could start this slow and if Shane gets annoyed Gabe could laugh it off. "I didn't feel like sleeping, but that was my first sermon." His muscles tensed as he watched for Shane's reaction.

"I didn't know that, I figured you guys just hadn't gone lately." Shane paused and sipped his hot chocolate. "Did it make sense to you? I mean, we all take it for granted everyone knows what's being talked about, but if you've never been there before it could be confusing. I mean, I didn't know what a parable was until I asked my mom."

Gabe wondered if he dared lead Shane in the direction he needed to get answers about the sermon. "Yeah. I didn't get what that was."

"Jesus used to tell stories to teach principles instead of telling

52

people flat out, do this or that. Parables are the stories He told."
Shane finished his drink and set the cup aside.

"I figured it was something like that. So what was he trying
to teach with that parable?" Gabe's hands shook inside his
mittens. How far could he push?

"Well, the lost sheep were sinners and everybody but Jesus
is a sinner, some worse than others. God still loves us, even if
we turn away and are really bad, God'll try and find a way to
bring us back to Him and He'll still love us."

"So what do we have to do to turn to God? I mean do we
have to make a big donation or do a special prayer?"

"Naw, just truly trust in Him in your heart."

"Trust in Him to do what?"

"Love you, guide you, want what's best for you."

"And if you truly trust in Him, then nothing will ever go
bad in your life?"

"I wish. If you mess up, you're still going to have to pay
the consequences, but if you're sorry for real, not because
you're supposed to be sorry, then God will forgive you."

"I don't get it. Give me a parable I'll understand." Gabe
watched Shane smile at his little joke. So far so good.

"If you don't study for a big test, you're still going to get
a bad grade. God doesn't change that, but if you're truly sorry
God will forgive you."

"That doesn't help much. Life will still be the pits." Gabe's
stomach rebelled at the let down from Shane's words.

"Yeah, well then study and it won't be as bad. The thing is,
no matter how bad it gets, God is there with you, giving you a
hug from the inside so you're never alone." Shane looked down
at his glove and picked at a loose thread. "I don't know, you
probably have so many friends that you aren't alone or lonely,
but if you ever get there, knowing God is standing beside
you, knowing the truth about you and wanting you to make it
through can be the difference in keeping going or giving up."

Shane flopped over and closed his eyes like he was sleeping.
Waves of thoughts crashed against Gabe's brain. "Shane, don't

you have lots of friend? I mean- there's Chuck and Kevin and Peter."

"They're buddies. We play video games and share music but I can't trust them with secrets or depend on them to help me. It always seems like everything is a competition and somebody has to win and somebody has to lose. I do have lots of really good friends; they just all have four feet. You're about the only two footed real friend I have."

Silence reigned in the makeshift shelter. Shane's words echoed his world. Other kids didn't want him to do well. The guys at school were always putting him down. In Shane's terms they had to win so he had to lose. For Shane, believing in God made this better? How?

Gabe flipped over onto his back "Okay, God, I'll give it a try. Please be with me on Monday when seeing Jasmine with Daniel makes me feel like a knife's been stabbed into my heart," he prayed to himself. Then- "Hey," Gabe said softly.

"What?" the word was muffled by Shane's hood and he hadn't opened his eyes.

"Thanks. I thought I was the only one without friends."

Shane opened his eyes and turned toward him. "You could get a lot of friends in the troop if you told my patrol what I just said."

"I won't trade a friend for a bunch of buddies. Besides that would make you my enemy."

"Jesus said we should to pray for our enemies as well as our friends. I tried praying that they'd fall down and break their necks, but Mom said she didn't think that was what Jesus meant."

Gabe had to laugh. "Thanks, I'd just as soon have you praying I pass algebra than that I break my neck. I'm clumsy enough to do that without your prayers."

"Okay, I'll pray you pass but if you really want to have that happen, ask my mom for help."

"She helped me once before but I don't want to bug her."

"You're not bugging her. She's a little weird and likes math. She does it for fun sometimes. And it'll get her out of my hair and checking my homework for once."

"Cool." Breathing seemed a little easier. Maybe life wasn't the total pits after all. "What do you do when people make you feel really bad?"

Remember at the troop meeting when I left the patrol and hung out with you?"

Gabe nodded. "Green -eyed monster time?"

"Yeah, I walk away."

"What if you can't get away?"

"Mom told me to think of the twenty-third psalm, 'The Lord is my shepherd I shall not want.' Only, don't tell her or she'll get all goofy, I was flipping through the Bible and I found a different one. It goes,' Answer me quickly Lord, my spirit fails. Save me from my enemies, I flee to you for refuge. Teach me to do your will for you are my God. Let your good spirit lead me on a level path.' About the time I get to that point, I realize how stupid and small the argument is and breathe. Then I feel warm inside and start to laugh and the other guy doesn't know what to do so they generally shut up and leave me alone."

Off in the distance Gabe heard the bell of one of the search dogs. He rolled over and got the toy out. "Where do I find that?"

"Psalm 143. Head's up, Babe's here."

Gabe made a mental note as Babe's loud barks echoed off the tarps and beat on his ears. Could he learn to laugh in Daniel's face? Would it make a difference? Well, it was worth a try.

Brian arrived and nodded. Gabe swung the cong out of hiding and felt the jerk all the way up to his armpits as the big dog dragged him out of the shelter and back into the cold wind.

CHAPTER 12

Gabe took a deep breath and yanked open the school door. Cold air flowed in behind him until the door closed with a thump. He didn't see either Jazz or Daniel. So far so good.

He opened his locker, dropped his pack on his toes, and went to hang up his coat. Suddenly, the door swung violently, revealing Daniel's smirk. The top of his pack was the only thing keeping it from shutting. Daniel's angry face slid between him and the portal.

Help, God.

"You're a real jerk, Turner."

Gabe inhaled and prayed, "Answer me quickly, God, I'm going down for the count."

"Daniel Case, you could have seriously injured Gabe with that foolish move. Do you have a problem?" Mr. Strickland stood a few steps away.

Daniel made a face. "Sorry Mr. Strickland, I tripped."

"That's not what it looked like. Please accompany me."

"This isn't over, Turner." Daniel's words hissed out softly. Gabe knew the teacher hadn't heard them in the noisy hallway.

Daniel turned back to Mr. Strickland with an innocent expression on his face. "Honest, Mr. Strickland, I just tripped, that's all."

"If that's true, then it should help to teach you not to tease Gabe about the times he trips. Come to think of it, about the only time he trips is when you're near by. You wouldn't be giving him a helping hand would you?"

Gabe watched Daniel's ears turn red as the boy walked away. Gabe couldn't make out the words but the whiny tone made him figured Daniel offered excuses. He turned back to the locker and hung his coat on the hook. His hands shook. That was close. Was that you God? No one has ever interfered before when Daniel pushed me around.

His hands stopped shaking along with the tingling in his face. Maybe God had watched out for him. He grabbed his English book and slammed the locker closed.

He dropped into his assigned seat and watched the other students hurry in. Jazz came in just before the bell rang. She glanced around the room, her bright hair swinging. Her gaze fell on him and her lips tightened, her eyes squinted and her nose wrinkled up. She turned and gazed toward Daniel's seat her expression softening. Gabe felt a pain in his chest. Even now, he would have given a lot to have her look at him that way.

"Everyone, please continue to work on your papers. I need to talk to a few people individually," Mr. Strickland said. He hurried around the room, returning the graded first drafts.

Gabe reached up and took the three pages. A big red "D" minus and "see me" scrawled across the top of the first page. Heat filled his face and he quickly curled up the sides of the pages so no one around him could see the grade.

Mr. Strickland finished handing out papers and motioned Gabe to come up to his desk. Gabe rolled the pages into a tube and hurried forward, careful not to trip on the packs and bags spilled into the aisle.

"This paper needs to be seven to ten pages. Your draft barely filled two and a half. " The teacher took the papers and spread them out on his desk. He used a pencil holder and a ruler to keep the sheets from rolling back up.

"I know, but I just don't know what else to say. Should I say the same thing over again a couple more times?"

"It's not just a question of volume but also of content.

You've stated a position, now you have to defend it."

"I thought I did."

"You didn't. The assignment is to write a persuasive paper. You need to talk the reader into agreeing with your point of view. Do some more research, find more evidence to support the argument you made and give me at least two more reasons to prove Scouting benefits boys and therefore society." Mr. Strickland stacked the pages together and handed them back.

Gabe returned to his seat and couldn't keep from glancing at her. She gave him a nasty smile. How can she be so mean? He slumped into his seat and closed his eyes. He swallowed hard to keep the pain inside instead of showing on his face. He had no idea what to write. Could, God put the words into his mind so Gabe could get a good grade?

He pictured being back at search practice and heard Shane's voice echoing off the blue tarps,

"If you don't study, God won't make it so you pass."

Wait a minute, the search team… Gabe pulled out his pen. A lot of what he learned about camping was helping in the search team. Could he use it as part of the arguments? He had talked about the scout law. Could he find something in the oath to use?

The bell rang and he gathered his papers. Ideas boiled around in his head. He rushed out the door to study hall. He had got to get this stuff down on paper before he forgot it.

Jazz blocked his path. "I thought you liked me, Turner."

"I thought I did, too."

What did she want? He tried not to notice the sweet scent coming from her hair, but her blonde curls almost brushed his chin.

"Well, you blew your chance of ever being my friend. After the way you threw those flowers at me, I'm going to tell everyone I know that you're a jerk and not to have anything to do with you. So if you end up with no friends, it's your own fault." She spun around and hurried away from him.

Gabe walked on to the study hall focusing on the floor a few steps in front of him. An ache radiated from his chest to his arms and up into his head as he relived the mocking laughter and cutting comments at the dance. All the good ideas evaporated from his brain. He sat through the study hall staring at a blank piece of paper.

*****

His stomach made a noisy rumble as he headed to the cafeteria line. He had been so hungry he hadn't been able to concentrate in his last class. Of course because it was math, it didn't matter if he concentrated or not. It just didn't make sense.

Three loaded hot dogs and a big glass of juice decorated his tray. He closed his eyes to savor the aroma curling around his nose before trying to find a seat. Suddenly, the tray flew out of his hands. A crash rang through the air as his tray hit the floor.

His eyes snapped open to see Daniel hurrying away with a self-satisfied smile on his face. Not again. Hey, God, where were you? Gabe sighed and collected what he could of the food off the floor. He tossed the big chunks onto the tray and emptied it into the trash can.

One of the monitors walked up behind him and bent down to mop the liquid up with a wad of paper towels. "This seems to be happening a lot, son. Do you have a problem with watching where you're going?"

Gabe toyed with telling. It'd be his word against Daniel's and Daniel's friends would claim Gabe lied. They'd done it the first time he'd gone to a monitor for help. He'd gotten off with a warning not to lie again or he'd get a detention. "No sir."

"Go jump line and get another meal so you have enough time to eat. I'll finish cleaning this up."

The man stood up at the same time as Gabe, whistled and waved. Gabe wished the floor would open and swallow him.

"Hey Agnes, let this boy cut in on the line," he yelled.

The woman nodded and motioned for Gabe to go. A few minutes later he had another full tray and just under five minutes left to eat. He plunked down at the closest table and shoveled food into his mouth.

"Oh, gross, Turner. You eat like a pig."

Jazz's words seemed to carry across the huge room. The students around him certainly stared. Before he could swallow, she had turned on her heel and flounced away. He could feel his face warm and he blinked his eyes to keep them from watering. Could he blame tears on the onions? A glance at the clock told him he had two minutes left. He let out the breath he'd been holding and grabbed the second dog. Might as well finish eating, nothing else seems to work. He guessed he shouldn't have said anything and a nice person wouldn't have thrown the flowers. She just made him so mad. He should have controlled his feelings like his Dad told him to do. It probably was his fault he didn't fit in. Would he ever learn how to do the cool thing instead of the dorky one? He didn't think even God could help him with that.

The bell rang and Gabe grabbed his tray. A quick flick of his wrist and he emptied it into the trash. He dropped it on the stack and joined the crush of students trying to get out the door. Great, now he was going to be late and Mrs. Amidon wouldn't accept late homework.

CHAPTER 13

Gabe slid into his seat for the last class of the day and dropped his books on the fake wood surface. Would this day never end? Glancing down, he saw the big red "F" on his persuasive paper sticking out of the top of his binder. He opened the folder to shove it back in only to spot the matching grade on the math quiz. He pushed the paper back into place and quickly closed it.

"Class, put away your books and take out a pencil and paper." Mrs. Hastings closed the door and walked to the front of the room. She reached down and gave a sharp tug on the open map hanging across the whiteboard. It rolled up swiftly to reveal the handwritten questions it had been hiding. "This is a true false quiz and you should be able to finish in ten minutes or less."

Gabe joined the collective groan and hurried to find a blank piece of paper. 'The two sides in the French and Indian war were the British and the French.' He tried to visualize last night's reading. That seemed to be correct, but then why would it have been named the 'French and Indian War?' He wrote false next to the number one.

"Put your pencils down and pass your papers forward."

No, I'm only on question eight and I left four and five blank. The boy behind him tapped Gabe's shoulder and handed up a stack of papers. Expelling a deep breath, Gabe added his paper to the pile and passed it forward.

Perfect, just perfect. Straight F's in every class for this day!

*****

Gabe turned and closed the front door before the swirling wind could rip it out of his hand. He stomped the snow from his feet while taking off his gloves. The bitter weather had numbed his face and it burned as it started to warm up, but it had been worth it. The neighbors had paid him to shovel their walks again and he had the last of the money to pay back his parents for the tux rental. Maybe now he could put that mess behind him.

"Hey, Dad," The house was way too quiet. "Are you home?"

"In the kitchen, Gabriel."

Gabriel? What'd I do now? He hung his snowy coat on a chair to dry and hurried down the hallway, grabbing the door jam to swing into the room. Both his parents were sitting at the table and neither of them looked happy. His feet stopped moving. The fleeting urge to turn around and go back outside churned through his brain and then left it empty.

"Sit down, son." His dad pushed a chair back from the table and tried to smile. His mom sniffed and peered into her coffee cup.

Gabe withdrew the money from his pocket as he slid into the chair. "I'm sorry I'm late. I shoveled walks on the way home. Here's the money I owe you."

His dad quietly picked up the crumpled wad of bills and smoothed them out on the table. He hesitated and then seemed to come to a decision. "I'm not surprised you paid us back. Even with all that happened, you took your responsibilities seriously. It makes it doubly hard to understand why you aren't paying attention in school. Don't you understand your first and most important job is to get good grades?"

"I am paying attention." How could he tell them about the "F" on his paper, now? They would ask why and he just couldn't tell them that he saw Jazz and Daniel together and his mind went blank.

"If you were, you'd be passing, not failing."

Gabe swallowed hard and looked first at his mom and then his Dad. They sat there watching him, waiting. "I'm sorry. I tried, but I just don't get this stuff, not even the dummy math. It doesn't make any sense."

"Why didn't you say something?" Dad asked.

"I don't know. I thought if I kept going and doing the homework, I'd get to the point where I understood something and could make up the bad grades."

"You're almost to the point of not being able to pass. If you can't pull all your averages up to a C, you're going to have to repeat this year."

Gabe went red hot and then ice started in his hands and feet and raced to his insides. "No. I can't do that. I can't go through this again. I'll drop out of school first."

"That's not an option. You're going to have to get your priorities straight. At this point your work with the search team is over for the rest of the semester and we're going to have to consider if you should also take a break from scouts."

"No, Dad, please don't. The only place I have any friends is at search practice and scouting." Gabe's throat felt like it had swelled shut as soon as the words came out of his mouth. He wasn't supposed to tell them, but tears started to flow and he couldn't stop them. He hung his head and pinched the bridge of his nose hoping the pain would make the crying stop.

Silence.

"Go to your room." The words were softly spoken but in the quiet they sounded like a shout.

Gabe stood and hurried to his sanctuary, closing the door behind him. He slumped to the floor and then dissolved fully into tears. The sobs welled up from his stomach and came out a terrible hoarse sound. He crawled to the bed and grabbed his pillow. He shoved his face into the cool fabric to muffle the noise. He couldn't stop. The pain just wouldn't stay inside anymore.

"Please, God, no. I finally have a friend. If I stop going to scouts and search practice, I'll lose him. Please, I can't do this. Please don't make me. Please, please help me. Please."

CHAPTER 14

The sobs began to slow. Gradually warmth flowed back into his body. He sat up, feeling as stiff and as sore as an old man. His cell phone buzzed softly from where it lay on his desk.

He picked it up, saw "1 message" and flipped the phone open.

"Yo, Gabe, this is Shane. Mom asked if your dad could pick me up and we could get out hiding before the rest of the team gets there on Sunday. She wants to run some aged problems for the dogs. You know there have to be several hours between the person going out and the dogs starting to look for them. Give me a call."

Instinctively, he hit the call back button. As soon as the first ring went off, he realized Shane would hear the tears in his voice. Before he could hit the end call, Shane picked up.

"Look, Shane, I don't think we can pick you up. Well, maybe my dad still can, but I can't go."

"Why, are you sick? You sound strange?"

He tried to think up a believable lie, but couldn't. "No, I'm in trouble and I need to stay home and study."

"What'd you do? Hit somebody?"

"Got straight F's. Look. I don't feel like talking about it. I just can't go. Okay?"

"Sure, it's okay. I'll tell Mom. It's too bad, Babe and Taz were really improving with you out to hide for them. You make a difference and everyone thought we could move up the testing date because of your work with the dogs. Is there anything I can do to help?"

"Take my algebra test for me?"

"Somehow I think they'd notice the height difference." Shane laughed.

A broken chuckle rattled out of Gabe's chest and almost turned into a sob.

"Is it just math that's the problem? 'Cause I know Mom would tutor you. She's sick enough to do quadratics for the fun of it." Shane said.

"No offense but that's weird. Besides it's everything. How is she at English papers and American history?"

"Actually, she's not bad but Dad likes to help with the papers and Brian helped me with history. He made it interesting instead of just memorizing a bunch of dates."

"Yeah but it's different with you."

"How so?"

"You're their kid."

"I'm no relation to Brian and I don't intend to change that. I refuse to accept balding genes from team members. When it comes to getting the dogs through their testing so we can take call outs, Mom, Dad and Brian'll do whatever is needed to get it done and I can tell you from the conversations I've overheard, you're needed."

"You really think they would tutor me?"

"Yup."

Was that God?

"Gabe, are you still there?"

"Yeah, sorry, I was just thinking."

"What, about how sorry you're going to be when they start whipping your brain into mush?"

"No, about whether or not this might be God's answer. I don't want to quit the search team and I really don't want to drop scouting and I didn't see any other way to go."

"No way; you can't drop scouts this close to your Eagle. That couldn't be the path God wants you to follow. Don't give up. I'll talk to Mom and maybe they can work out a tutoring schedule with your dad at scouts tomorrow night."

Gabe flipped the phone shut ending the call. The lump of tears in his stomach disappeared. "That was You, wasn't it? You are out there and You do care about me. Thanks. Now could you please help me convince my parents to do this?" Gabe said out loud.

He dropped his pillow back on the bed and soft footed it down the hallway. His parents were still in the kitchen talking and he could just make out their words if he strained his ears.

"You know, Rich, he may not be able to learn." His mother's voice sounded so sad.

"Why? Because that's what the doctors said?" His dad answered.

What doctors? Is there something wrong with me Mom and Dad haven't told me?

"Like it or not, that bout with chicken pox as a baby had its repercussions on Gabe," his mom said.

"Don't you think I know that? I was there, too Corrine. I was the one holding Shellie when she died."

Who was Shellie? Gabe didn't remember having chicken pox.

"All I'm saying is we can't be too hard on him. He's always so responsible; it's not like him to deliberately fail at school. His grades have never been very good and it may just be that he can't do the work and not that he won't. We're the ones responsible, letting that woman bring a disease into our house. We can't take it out on him."

It was said it didn't pay to eavesdrop; now Gabe knew why. He cleared his throat to warn his parents of his presence and walked into the room.

"Look Mom, Dad, this is my fault. I probably haven't been paying as much attention as I should and I am behind. But, I really don't want to stop scouting or working with the dogs."

He scrubbed at a dried spill on the floor in front of him with his toe. What were the right words?

He looked directly into his Dad's eyes. "This is my mistake and it's up to me to fix it. Just reading the texts over and over again isn't going to help me learn. I need somebody to teach me, one on one. I just talked to Shane and he said his parents and Brian would tutor me if I kept coming to search practice." He sucked a deep wad of air into his lungs and let it out. "They won't charge me but you may have to drive me to them a lot."

His dad stared at him for what seemed an eternity, and then looked down at his hands without saying a word. Gabe walked to the table and covered his Dad's hand with his own. "Please Dad, let me try and fix this."

"Do you really think you can learn the material with a tutor?"

"I want to try."

His dad leaned back in the chair and smiled. "Okay, I'll call the O'Haras and get the ball rolling." Dad reached out one hand and ruffled Gabe's hair. "I'm really proud of you son, pass or fail, I wouldn't trade you for anyone."

The ice ball in the pit of his stomach suddenly dissolved. He glanced over and saw tears running down his mom's face. He turned to give her a hug as his father walked to the telephone and dialed.

"Hello, Jim? It's Rich." A pause.

"Shane's brought you up to date, already?" Gabe could hear Mr. O'Hara's voice, but not the words.

"Sounds like a plan. I'll tell Gabe." His dad listened for a moment. "I owe you big time for this." More unintelligible words, then his dad laughed and hung up.

"What'd he say?" Gabe could feel his breath burning in his lungs.

"Get a good night's sleep because starting tomorrow they own you until you finish school."

"Huh?"

"Mrs. O'Hara will be waiting for you at scouts. She's going to review your math homework while you take a test. Mr. O'Hara wants to see your last three English papers and Brian will take you home with him on Sunday to work on history. Expect to be picked up every night by one of them, tutored and brought home around ten."

"Oh Rich, that's late," his mom said.

His dad turned to his mom and smiled. "He'll survive."

"And you," his dad had turned back to Gabe. "Mrs. O'Hara says every time you mess up she's going to make you do a page of geometry theorems and then make you hide in dense brush for the dogs."

"But I'm taking algebra and I practically have to crawl to get through dense brush."

"She knows. She wanted you to have some added incentive." His dad laughed out loud.

Gabe groaned and pictured getting stuck on thorns and having brambles rip hair from his head. "Can I buy a machete?"

CHAPTER 15

Gabe stood at the back of the patrol line and watched Chuck in action. The patrol had lined up in a perfectly straight line with the boys evenly spaced. Chuck walked down the line inspecting the other boys.

"Peter, where's your handbook?" he asked.

"I forgot it."

"Great, now we lose points and may not get the patrol award for the month. If we don't win, it'll be on you." Chuck said.

He walked down the line to the next boy. "Kevin, tuck in your shirt. Your patrol patch is on the wrong sleeve. Don't you know anything?"

Kevin appeared to be inspecting the floor. Gabe could barely make out his mumbled "Sorry."

Gabe looked at the other patrols. They were all lined up but the similarity ended there. Some boys chatted with their neighbors and others traded baseball cards. Two others compared song lists on their iPods. The lines reminded him of snakes the way they zigged and zagged as the boys clustered together. A sigh escaped him. Scouting was about doing things right, but it was also about having fun while you did them.

Chuck had reached the end of the line and looked up at Gabe. "What do I do? They don't seem to care if we're the best or not."

"Scouting is all about team work and learning and helping each other. This isn't the Marine Corps. Relax a little. The patrol awards are supposed to be fun, not a weapon to make the other scouts do what you want."

"What I want is to be an Eagle Scout." Chuck said.

"Why?" Gabe asked.

Chuck rolled his eyes and shook his head. "What do you mean 'why'? Because I want everyone to know I'm the best so it'll look good on my college applications and job resumes."

"You've got it all wrong. An Eagle Scout is someone who does his best, can be counted on to get the job done and can motivate other people. When you get to your Eagle project, you have to direct other people, not do all the work yourself." Gabe said.

"That's what I'm doing."

"No you're trying to make people do things to make you look good. What's in it for them?"

"We all share in the award."

"Getting the patrol award isn't going to keep the boys coming back to meetings if all that happens is they get told how bad they are. If they don't come to meetings you'll end up the leader of nobody and attendance counts the most. If you really want to win the award, you have to make it so everyone is working toward that goal instead of you pushing them." Gabe stopped to catch his breath.

The glazed over look in Chuck's eyes made it clear the boy had tuned him out. He opened his mouth to continue but shouts of "fall in" interrupted him. Chuck hurried to his place at the front of the line.

"Scouts, attention." The Troop Leader yelled and stood ramrod straight. "Scouts, salute."

Four boys marched forward, one carrying the American flag another carrying the Troop flag.

"Post the colors." The Leader said.

Gabe recited the Pledge of Allegiance and the Scout Oath but his mind focused on Chuck. How could he explain the difference between pushing and motivating?

The boys split off with different adult leaders to work on merit badges. Gabe made sure all the boys under his guidance had a task or training to keep them busy. He collected his school books where he'd dumped them and looked for Mr. and Mrs. O'Hara. Mrs. O'Hara smiled and jerked her head toward the empty room across the hall. Time for him to show them just how dumb he really was.

"Okay, Gabe," Mr. O'Hara said, "Let me have your last three papers and the rubrics sheets for each."

Gabe fished them out of a pocket in his notebook. He could feel his face burning at the sight of the two "Fs" and a "D" scrawled in red on the front pages. He waited for some comment, but Mr. O'Hara took them, smiled and started reading the first paper.

"My turn," Mrs. O'Hara said."Pull up a chair."

Gabe sat beside her.

"Hand over your homework and the math book."

He had used the homework to mark the list of problems in the book.

"Is the math assignment completed?"

Yes."

She took it and handed him a sheet of paper. "This is a test and it isn't," she said,"Math builds on principles and rules. If somewhere along the way you missed some rules most of what you do from there on will be wrong. I need to find out if there are some basic things you don't understand."

"I don't understand any of it. My brain can't handle numbers. It's even worse when the problems have letters instead of numbers." There was no point in lying. She'd realize how stupid he was real quick.

"How are you with money? Do you have trouble making change or figuring out how much several items cost?" she asked.

"No, money is easy. It's important."

"From now on when you see a number, pretend you're talking about money. And if the formula has letters substitute numbers, so for "a" write two, "b' write three and so on."

Gabe took the test from her and began answering the questions. The room was so quiet he could hear the clock on the front wall ticking. The problems on her test weren't that hard and using the dollar and number substitution trick made some of them really easy.

"I'm done."

"Good. In looking over your homework it looks like we have to go over the multiplication of signs, but beyond that you understood the concepts from this section of the book." She looked up at the clock. "It's almost time to fall back in. Let me look over this test and I'll have a place for us to start tomorrow night."

Mr. O'Hara walked back over to them. "I see what's happening with your papers. Part of the problem is you aren't following the directions to get the points."

"I don't understand."

"The teacher is very clear on what he wants. Page length, number of arguments, and content are all clearly defined. I can see where you think you've addressed them. I'll start showing you why it didn't work, tomorrow night." He smiled at Gabe. "This is an easy problem to fix. You're on the right track, but we just need to move you further along."

"Do you really think so?"

Faint shouts of "fall in" reached his ears and he could see boys lining up across the hall. Gabe collected his books and got into line just as the color guard retrieved the colors.

Most of the boys had left. Gabe retrieved his coat. Where was Dad? He angled his head so he could see out the doorway and across the hall. There was his father talking to the O'Haras. As he started join them, his Dad's words froze him in place.

"Are you sure?" his dad asked. "The doctors were pretty certain that the case of chicken pox he had as a toddler had caused permanent brain damage and slowed his ability to learn."

Mrs. O'Hara shook her head from side to side. "Listen Rich, I'm no doctor, but I know when someone can do math and when they can't. I would guess some where around third grade he either missed a lot of school or the teacher had difficulty presenting math concepts. He just needs some basics. Those missed concepts are preventing him from understanding the next steps."

"I have to agree," Mr. O'Hara said. "A little polish and understanding of how to identify the requirements of the project and he'll be knocking the heck out of the curve."

Gabe stumbled backwards into one of the small classrooms.

Doctors said that he had brain damage? Why didn't Mom and Dad tell him? Is that why he didn't fit in, because his brain was whacked? How did he get chicken pox anyway? Why didn't he remember? Does this mean he was never going to be normal?

"There you are." His dad poked his head in the doorway and smiled. "Are you ready to go home?

Gabe nodded. He didn't trust his voice right now. He tightened his hold on his books and headed up the stairs to the parking lot. He needed to get to his room and think.

CHAPTER 16

"Who wants to attempt the next problem?" Mrs. Amidon asked.

Gabe read through the problem. That's one of the math codes, minus plus minus. I can do this one. He shot his hand into the air.

"Gabe." Mrs. Amidon said.

Gabe stood and walked to the whiteboard. Kathy turned from her problem and handed him the marker with a smile. A week ago he would have been running for the rest room. Not today. He had this one nailed! He looked at the problem.

A squared minus nine; factor into the components. Okay — "a" times "a" is "a" squared. That was easy. The chalk made a painful squeak as he quickly wrote the answer. He turned and looked at Mrs. Amidon. He knew that he hadn't messed this one up. The teacher smiled and nodded her head yes. He did it. Gabe could feel the grin plastered on his face as he walked back to his seat. His stomach turned cartwheels- the good kind.

"Okay, that's the last problem." Mrs. Amidon walked toward the front of the room. The homework assignment is page one seventy –eight. Do all the odd problems."

Gabe made a note in his assignment book as a groan went up around the classroom.'

"Hey God, thanks. I suppose there's a special way to say this and I'm still messing up, but thanks, I actually had fun in math. Thanks for weird Mrs. O'Hara and her math codes."

"However, Tom, Alexis, Kathy and Gabe, since you were brave enough to come to the board and did all the problems correctly, you do not have to do the homework unless you want extra credit," the teacher said.

All right. So Gabe could do the homework and bring his grade up some more.

The bell rang releasing everyone for the day.

Gabe grabbed his books and hurried for his locker. He had to get home and get ready for the campout this weekend with the troop. He would try working with Chuck this whole weekend. But if he couldn't get him to stop bossing and being the king of sarcasm, Gabe would need to go to Mr. C and have him step in.

$$*****$$

Gabe climbed out of the truck and grabbed an armload of gear to haul up to the cabin. He glanced over and saw Chuck standing by another truck pointing and calling orders out to the patrol. Out of the corner of his eye he saw Shane and Peter disappear around the back of one truck empty handed and going in the wrong direction. Although smaller than Peter, Shane's arm was around his shoulders in a comforting manner. What was up with those two?

Gabe walked up behind Chuck. The younger boy had placed his hands on his hips and frowned at the people around him.

"The best way to lead is by example," Gabe said.

Chuck whirled to face him, anger apparent in his expression. "So I'm supposed to do all the work and then share the credit?"

"Sometimes. Sometimes someone else does most of the work and shares the credit with you. Scouting is a give and take situation, no one gives all the time and no one takes all the time." Gabe shifted the load in his arms. "Come on, I'll give you a hand."

Chuck made a face and picked up two bags of groceries and struggled up the slushy path in front of Gabe. He slipped once and would have gone down if Gabe hadn't been able to brace Chuck's feet with the side of his boot. Once inside he deposited his burden and collapsed on his bunk to catch his breath. A few minutes later, Peter and Shane walked in carrying just their own gear.

"Peter, Shane." Chuck called out. "Since you two are too good to help hauling stuff up to the cabin, you have KP for the entire weekend."

Peter stiffened as if he'd been slapped. Shane patted him on the back and steered him to an open bunk. "That's fine. We'll take care of it."

Chuck gave them another scowl and moved over to the cracker barrel, the big blue action packer, to grab some snacks.

Gabe watched Peter and Shane, trying to read what was going on. If he didn't know better, he'd swear Peter had been crying. Peter stretched out on his sleeping bag, put on his headphones and laid on his bunk facing the wall and away from the room. With thirty boys and ten men all sharing the same space, it was as close as anyone got to privacy.

Quietly Gabe walked over to Shane's bunk. He pretended to be laying out his sleeping bag, but his eyes were closed and his lips moved silently. Gabe gently tapped his arm, Shane's eyes flashed open and for a second he looked ticked, then he smiled.

"I thought you were Chuck."

Gabe shook his head and spoke softly so his voice would carry only as far as Shane's ears. "What's going on? Is there something I should know about?"

Shane glanced over at Peter's still form and then at two rowdy boys pretending to wrestle nearby. "Yes, but not here. I promised Pete I'd keep it to myself. I'll tell you after the camp out. It may be over then anyway and not be a big deal."

Gabe rolled the words around in his head. Trusting Shane was a no brainer. He nodded and joined the cracker barrel group. Shane spent a few more minutes in his bunk then came and sat quietly next to Gabe. Each person took a turn trying to get a spoon to stick to his face. Of course as soon as they laughed the spoon fell off so each person worked their best weird expressions to get everyone else to laugh. Finally, the stories and jokes were done and Mr. C ordered lights out.

*****

Gabe stepped out of the cabin and joined the adult leaders as they planned the day's activities. He needed to see which projects would most benefit the patrol he guided. He signed them up for the group to build shelters with lashings and downed branches. It would satisfy all the knot tying requirements they would need for rank advancement. With a smile on his lips he walked back inside, almost getting bowled over by Kevin, running out the door. "Hey, watch where you're going!"

He stepped inside to the smell of burnt food and the sound of raised voices.

"I've had it with both of you." Chuck screamed at Peter and Shane. "He ruined it and he's going to eat it."

"Stop it." Shane protested and gently pushed Peter behind him and away from the hot and dangerous pan of burnt oatmeal. "He didn't mean it. He didn't know that it had to be stirred."

"Quit defending him. You're just sucking up to people so they'll vote you patrol leader and take away my authority. You want to prevent me from being an Eagle so you can tell people you're better than me. Mom told me to watch out for you, you're just like your mother." Chuck's face had turned beet red. He grabbed up the handle of the pan and tried to force Shane's face into the hot goop. "Well, if he's not eating it, you are."

Gabe lunged across the room, praying that he would get there in time. Shane moved so fast, he'd never seen anyone move in that way before. One second Chuck had the pan in one hand and the back of Shane's head in the other. The next second the pan crashed to the floor and Shane had Chuck in a head lock, his face pressed into the log wall.

"That's enough." Mr. C's voice cracked through the noise. "Shane, let go of Chuck."

Gabe watched Shane hesitate. His eyes were pea-green and he breathed hard. With a violent shove he let go, pushed away from Chuck, and turned to walk out the door.

Gabe looked at Mr. C. and followed his nod to go after Shane. In the coolness outside it was unnaturally quiet. All the boys had gone inside to see the cause of the commotion. A flash of orange caught his eye and he hurried off to the side where Shane sat on a stump, snapping a stick into pieces with his hands. Gabe couldn't believe how calm his friend was, then he saw how Shane's hands shook and the tears running down his face.

"Am I getting thrown out of Boy Scouts for this? Is he going to call my dad to come get me?" His voice would have been hard, had there not been tears in it.

Gabe knelt down in front of him. "Of course not. If they try, I'll quit, too." Shane's shoulders shook. Gabe could hear him trying to swallow the sobs.

"Dad told me I'm nobody's punching bag and someday I'd need to defend myself, so he taught me some stuff he learned as a bouncer." Shane swallowed with an audible gulp. "It was fun to learn, but it was hard to have to use it."

"I've never been so scared in my life. I thought Chuck was going to stick your face in that hot stuff before I could stop him."

"I sure hope God counts this like the time Jesus got mad at the moneychangers and threw them out of the temple otherwise I'm cooked. I don't feel sorry about stopping Chuck."

Gabe wasn't sure how to answer. This whole God thing was new to him and he didn't have a clue what to tell the younger boy. What moneychangers? I need to distract him, the others will be out soon and I don't want them to see him crying. "Look before anyone comes out, what's going on with Peter?"

Shane sat back and picked up his stick. He swiped at his eyes with a sleeve and took a quick glance over his shoulder at the cabin before going back to breaking off pieces. "The reason Peter's dad and mine stayed home this weekend is that Peter's mom has been told she has cancer. They're doing an operation on her to cut it out. Dad stayed to be there for Peter's dad if things went bad. Peter wasn't supposed to know, but he overheard them talking and he's frightened for his mom. He wants to be home, not here."

Gabe felt like he'd been kicked in the stomach. What if something like that happened to his mom? What would he have said if he'd come to Gabe instead of Shane?

"What did you say to him?"

"God would be there with her and if we prayed it'd all be all right."

"Is that the way it works?" Gabe asked.

"Sort of, but sometimes God has other plans we don't know about. What if he's going home to no Mom at all? I didn't know what else to say and I had to say something to make him feel better."

"So you were praying when we talked last night?"

Shane nodded.

"We need to tell Mr. C. He'll know what to do." Gabe said.

"Is that before or after he bawls me out?" Shane asked.

Gabe didn't have an answer. Fighting wasn't taken lightly in scouts and whatever Mr. C decided the troop would support. They'd have the choice of accepting it or quitting. Was God trying to tell Gabe not to get his Eagle? They needed God, but so did Peter's mom. If God did not have time for all of them, hopefully he would be with her and heal her. That was what mattered the most.

Gabe heard the cabin door slam and saw scouts and leaders walking out into the clearing in front of the cabin. His dad stood there with the others for a second, slowly turning in a big circle. When he faced Gabe he started walking toward him.

"Heads up, my dad is coming." Gabe wanted to be sure Shane had his tears under control.

"Mr. C wants you and Shane inside. The rest of the leaders are taking the others on a hike."

CHAPTER 17

Gabe watched the others hike off in formation down the trail. Shane still sat on the stump staring at the ground and breaking twigs.

"C'mon, we might as well go inside."

Gabe led the way into the cabin. Mr. C, Chuck and Peter sat at the table in the kitchen, the oatmeal goop untouched on the floor. Shane sat down next to Mr. C and across from Chuck. Gabe took the chair on the other side of Shane.

"Chuck and Shane, what happened here today was dangerous and unacceptable. I'd like to understand what started this and try and get to the bottom of it once and for all." Mr. C said. "Chuck, you get to start."

Chuck pointed a finger at Shane. "It's all his fault. He's always trying to suck up to people and won't support me as patrol leader."

Gabe saw Shane's eyes changing color and grabbed his leg under the table. He needed to stay calm.

Chuck sucked in a deep breath and started to talk again. "This is a perfect example with the oatmeal. He let Peter burn the breakfast for the whole patrol and then wouldn't make him pay the consequences of his mistake."

"Shoving anyone's face into hot oatmeal is dangerous." Shane said.

"See, he's interrupting. Don't I get to finish?" Chuck faced Mr. C. with an injured expression.

"Shane, you'll get your turn to speak. Let Chuck finish." Mr. C. nodded to Chuck.

"Since he prevented Peter from owning up to what he did, I figured Shane wanted to take Peter's place, so I was going to feed him the burnt food. Next thing I know, my right hand is numb and he's grinding my face into the wall while he's trying to break my arm. I wasn't going to hurt him but he sure hurt me." Chuck rubbed his elbow and looked about ready to cry.

Gabe watched Mr. C.'s face trying to gage the impact Chuck had made. Mr. C. should played poker; one could not tell from his face what he thought. The silence stretched until Gabe wanted to say something, anything, to make the quiet go away. Just as he opened his mouth, Mr. C. turned to Shane.

"Okay Shane, it's your turn to talk."

"Chuck thinks he has to push everyone around and give orders because he's patrol leader. None of the other patrols have to meet all his special rules. We've all tried to go along, even when he screams at us and hands out assignments as punishments, but this time he went too far."

"See he admits it, going behind my back and undermining my authority." Chuck shouted while partially rising from his chair.

"Sit down. You had your turn to talk, now its Shane's turn." Mr. C. didn't even raise his voice or move in his chair. "If you've been putting up with Chuck, what changed today?"

Shane shifted in his chair. "Today it got dangerous. He was waving that pot of hot goop around and then he grabbed the back of my head and started pushing my face toward it. I didn't want to get burned, so I hit a nerve in his hand to make it go numb and put him in a wrist-lock until he calmed down. I didn't hit him or try and hurt him and I could have. I'm not going to get burned because he decided to throw a hissy fit."

"See I told you he wanted to take over from me." Chuck pointed out.

"Peter, Gabe, do you have anything to add?"

Gabe shook his head no. There wasn't anything left to say. He looked at Peter who also shook his head from side to side.

"Shane, you clean up the floor and the pan and I expect them to be spotless. Gabe, you stay here and watch, but don't let Peter help Shane. Don't you help him either."

Gabe looked at Mr. C. How could he blame Shane? Chuck had a big grin on his face and crossed his arms over his chest as he stared at Shane.

"Chuck, come outside with me." Mr. C stood and walked toward the door. Chuck, a few steps behind Mr. C., turned to make a face at Shane.

"Do a good job, Shane, I'll be back to inspect your work and I don't expect it to be good enough."

"No, you won't. We're going to discuss if you remain part of the Ravens Patrol at all. If you do, it won't be as patrol leader." Mr. C. put a hand on Chuck's back and gently helped him out the door.

Gabe watched Shane scrub the oatmeal pan. The rest of the troop returned, muddy, laughing and talking. The troop broke down into patrols and started to pass out food. The boys piled inside and slapped sandwiches together.

Peter came over and got out a frying pan, bread, cheese and butter. "How do I make grilled cheese with a frying pan?"

Gabe stood beside him. "Spread butter on a slice of bread, put it butter-side down in the pan. Put the cheese on top and then another slice of bread. Watch it close, these sandwiches burn easily."

Gabe stepped back and watched Peter's progress. The boy looked awkward as he tried to manipulate the sandwiches with a big spatula. Some of the sandwiches were under done and some over done but all were edible.

Chuck came back in and sat with the Cougars Patrol. They handed him a peanut butter sandwich and kept on talking.

Peter left two sandwiches on the counter and motioned to them and then pointed to Shane and to Gabe. Gabe nodded. That was lunch-or was it breakfast?

Mr. C. walked over to Shane and looked at the pot. "That's good, Shane. Go eat your lunch."

Shane rinsed the pot, dried his hands and walked outside without a glance at his sandwich. Gabe watched him go. Should I follow him or give him some space? He looked at Mr. C. and realized that he was being watched.

"Guiding those younger and more inexperienced than you isn't easy, is it?" Mr. C. asked softly.

"Why did you punish him?"

"Never, ever let one scout hurt another and go unpunished." Mr. C. turned to walk away.

"Wait." Gabe grabbed the Troop Master's arm and pulled him toward a quiet corner of the kitchen. "Have you talked to Peter's Dad?"

"What about?"

"Peter's mom."

Mr. C. looked around the room quickly and then back at Gabe. "What do you know about it?"

"Peter knows she's being operated on. He's worried and he wants to go home." Gabe said. "Look, this camp out is a bust for the Ravens Patrol anyway. Can we just pack it in and let my dad drive us home?"

Mr. C. thought for a while, and then shook his head no. "There isn't enough room in your truck and all the patrol will remember is the fight. If we send them home now they'll be turned off about scouting."

"What do we do, then?"

"We work them the rest of the day on everything they need to get a rank advancement. Get your dad and any of the adult leaders you need and work their tails off. By Sunday have their books ready to be signed off and start prepping them for their first Court of Honor. Make a big deal out of it and the fight will be old news. After the Court of Honor they can elect a new patrol leader instead of having a special election." Mr. C. walked over and picked up one of the cold sandwiches. "Eat your lunch; you're going to need it."

Gabe watched him go then picked up his sandwich and walked to the window. Mr. C sat on a stump next to Shane, talking. Gabe watched until he saw Shane finally take a bite of his sandwich. Gabe stuffed the remains of his own sandwich into his mouth and navigated to his bunk to grab his handbook. He walked over to his dad and some of the other adult leaders. He opened the book to the Tenderfoot requirements. He had the rest of the day to get the patrol through ten activities.

"Adult leaders, I need some help."

CHAPTER 18

"Gabe, come in here." Dad shouted from the kitchen.

Gabe hurried down the hallway in his stocking feet, sliding the last stretch. He grabbed the door jamb to stop his forward momentum and swing through the kitchen doorway. His dad sat at the table, looking at a paper in his hand. His mom sat across from him, sipping tea.

"What's up?"

"I have your grades, here."

His Dad's solemn expression made Gabe's heart skip a beat. He had checked the school listing, he had passed everything. Was there a mistake?

Gabe slipped into an empty chair before his knees gave out. "The website had all passing grades."

"Passing?" Dad turned to Mom, "Do you hear that, passing?"

His dad turned back to him with a huge smile, "You did better than passing, five B's and three C's. I couldn't be prouder if I were twins. You did it."

He looked at his mom and he realized that she had been using the cup to hide her smile.

"We're so proud of you."

Gabe felt his heart start beating again and the heat in his face as the blood rushed back. "I owe the search team big time. Everything they said made sense. It's easy to pass a test when things make sense."

"That's the truth," Dad said, "I called and we're taking them all out to dinner after practice Sunday as a thank you."

"Isn't that going to cost a lot?" Gabe mentally pictured everyone sitting around a restaurant table and started multiplying in his head. It didn't take long to realize the bill would be huge.

"It's peanuts compared to the alternative of failing school and dropping from Scouts. Let your mom and me worry about it."

"I've got the rest of the money I earned shoveling snow, if you need it." He got up and walked back to his room. His own reflection made him halt as he entered his room and saw his own smile. I did it.

*****

"Are the dogs going to be okay in the trucks while we eat?" Gabe whispered to Shane.

"Yeah, it's cool and overcast and the windows are partway open. The handlers will take turns coming out to check them. The dogs'll catch a nap and sniff for leftovers when we come out."

A waitress grabbed a handful of menus and motioned them to follow her. Gabe looked at the menu and tried to find the least expensive dinner.

"What're you going to get?"

"I guess the angel hair pasta alfredo." Shane leaned forward and looked down the table. "Hey Mr. Turner, do you think you could teach them how to make rattlesnake pasta? I don't see it on the menu."

"Yuck, I don't think too many people want to eat snake." Brian's wife, Anna said.

Gabe grabbed the sides of his chair to keep from falling to the floor. When he scrubbed the laughter tears from his face he realized that the others weren't in much better shape.

"Anna, it really wasn't snake. It was Italian sausage," Gabe's dad said.

"Then why did you tell me I let dinner get away, when the

snake made me scream?"

Gabe threw a hand over his mouth to catch the soda spewing out. The rest ran down his windpipe and he coughed and gasped for breath while Shane pounded on his back. Answer that one, Dad.

Gabe's mom looked around the table. "What am I missing?"

Mrs. O'Hara swallowed her iced tea. "Remember when we brought in the trainer from the East Coast to help us?"

His mom nodded.

"Anna brought Babe over so Brian could come straight to training from work. She tied Babe to a tree and screamed loud enough to break eardrums when she almost stepped on a grass snake." Mrs. O'Hara gave his dad and Mr. O'Hara a reproachful look. "Of course everyone came running thinking it had been an emergency. As soon as they found out it was nothing serious they decided to have some fun at Anna's expense." She shook her head and pointed at his dad and Mr. O'Hara. "Those two didn't miss a beat and immediately convinced Anna we actually were going to eat snake. When she came back for dinner and found out we were having rattlesnake pasta, she refused to eat no matter who told her it was really sausage."

The waitress moved to their table, a pad in one hand and a pen in the other.

"May I take your order?"

She stepped over to Shane and he opened his mouth. Gabe saw the mischief on the kid's face and grabbed his arm. Shane let out a theatrical sigh and ordered the angel hair pasta.

Mr. O'Hara raised his glass of iced tea, "Okay, everyone, here's to Gabe, an important player in getting the team operational." Gabe couldn't distinguish which cheer came from which person. People at nearby tables were all looking at them. He tried to slide down in his chair and under the table so no one could see him blush.

"Forget it buddy, you're too big to hide, so now you're stuck as an official team member." Shane's smile took the bite out of his words.

"Gabe, what are you going to do for an Eagle project?" Brian asked.

"Well, I was trying to think about what I could do for the church. I got an idea from the rummage sale but I don't know if it's possible."

His dad looked up from his burger. "Remember, it can't be for the troop. Eagle projects have to benefit the community."

"I know, and I think this will help more than the troop." Gabe took a sip of soda and swallowed. "The church parking lot is used for a lot of things like bake sales, rummage sales, bike safety training, and even construction projects. Any electricity that's needed for coffee pots, crock pots or even power tools always comes from the garage, but, there's only one plug on the garage light socket and people are always tripping breakers. What if my project ran more power out there and put in a breaker box and plugs?"

Gabe held his breath. This idea had been dancing around in his mind for the last few weeks. He hadn't had the courage to say anything before this.

Brian looked at Mr. Turner and Mr. O'Hara. "Will the town let a bunch of kids play with electricity?"

"Until the system is energized, they aren't in any danger," Mr. O'Hara said, "It's a big project. You'd have to come over and let me teach you how to do load calculations, look things up in the code books and draw up the plans."

"I don't see how he can do that," his mom said, "I mean we needed all your help to get him through school. How can he figure out electricity when he has trouble learning?"

"He doesn't have trouble learning. It was pretty clear as soon as I tutored him." Mrs. O'Hara took another sip of her iced tea.

"I'd have to agree with that." Brian said, "Most of what I taught him was memorization of dates and names. Once I put it into context and gave him some tricks to remember dates he had great recall."

"That's not what the doctors said." Mom answered.

Silence hammered Gabe into his chair. He couldn't believe she was saying this in front of everyone. He kept hearing about doctors. "What doctors?"

His mom flushed and glanced down at her plate. "It was a long time ago. You were just a toddler and you got chicken pox. The fevers were horrible and the doctors told us you would probably have trouble learning."

"I don't remember having chicken pox."

No one at the table spoke for an instant.

"Why didn't you tell me before now?" Pain ripped up from his stomach and settled behind his eyes. He closed them against the agony. His breath burned his lungs and whistled out his lips.

Tears welled up in his mother's eyes. "I..I.."

"Corrine, did Gabe miss a lot of school in third or fourth grade?" Mrs. O'Hara asked.

"Yes." She dabbed at her eyes with a napkin. "He uh, had strep throat about four times in third grade. It seemed like he was home sick more than he was in school that year."

Gabe opened his eyes. Mr. O'Hara and Brian nodded and smiled.

"I really didn't see any issues with retaining knowledge or Gabe's ability to understand." Mr. O'Hara said

"You didn't?"

Mr. O'Hara looked around at the others at the table and then smiled at Gabe. "I think we all saw the same thing. Missed basic principles, most of which are taught in third or fourth grade. I figured either he missed a lot of school or had a poor teacher."

Gabe grinned, "Does that mean I'm not brain dead?"

"No, Gabe- not at all.Of course that puts you on the hook to get good grades and succeed academically. No more excuses." Mrs. O'Hara answered him, but she looked at his mom. Gabe looked in the same direction; his mom smiled and cried at the same time.

"I don't know, Mom." Shane slipped over in his chair away from Gabe. "You haven't seen him in the morning at a camp out."

"Look who's talking?" Gabe swung his arm around to tickle Shane's ribs. "If we didn't have to wear uniforms at camp outs, you'd end up wearing your sleeping bag."

Shane ducked and the whole table laughed.

"Well, I guess that answers it," Dad said and took a sip of soda. "Looks like wiring the church garage is your Eagle project."

CHAPTER 19

Gabe adjusted his uniform sash and checked to make sure none of the merit badges were loose. He thought, "I wish we were doing this in either the troop's church or mine. At least it would be familiar. Still, it 's a church, so you are around here, aren't you God?" He tried to sip from the can of soda that he held but his hand shook so badly, he set it aside.

All he needed was to spill cola on his shirt.

His dad leaned against the white painted wall next to him. "That's the way I feel every time I walk into a church." Gabe spun to look at his Dad. The twinkle in his eye told him that his dad was teasing him.

"Don't worry, this is scouts. These people want all the boys here to be a success."

A slender man with a bald head wearing a scout leader uniform stepped out of the interview room. He carried a leather notebook with the Scouting fleur de lis engraved on the cover.

"Scout Gabriel Turner?"

Gabe inhaled and stepped forward.

"Here, sir." He picked up his project plan book and followed the man into the room.

"Be with me now God: I can't do this without you," he prayed silently. As the door closed he saw his dad sit down in one of the lobby chairs and give him a thumbs up and a smile.

"Have a seat, son. We need to finish up some paperwork before we get started."

The man nodded to a chair and then stepped away.

"I wish Dad could be in here with me," he said to himself.

Gabe lowered his body onto the seat and tried to sit up straight. Three men in uniform sat at the table across from him and pulled out papers, removing clips and shuffling the order.

A man wearing gold rimmed glasses smiled at him.

"While we're getting organized, why don't you tell us a little about yourself?"

Gabe swallowed hard. "Well, I'm fifteen and a freshman at Indian Creek High School. I've been in scouts since I turned twelve and crossed over from webelos."

What else should he say?

The bald man put his papers down and faced Gabe. "Tell us a little about your friends."

Shane's smiling face came to mind. He felt his lips curving in an answering smile.

"My best friend is a younger scout, named Shane. He just moved up this year. We have a lot of fun helping train search and rescue dogs. He's a real pint size tornado and always smiles. We spend almost every Sunday together, either training dogs or going to church."

"Did you meet him at church?"

"No sir, at scouts. His family invited me to go to church with them after he joined the troop."

"How do your parents feel about you going to a different church than them?"

"My dad and Shane's dad are friends. Mom and Dad don't mind; they know I'm okay with them."

The man with the gold rimmed glasses spoke again. "You said you train search and rescue dogs. Tell us about it."

"Shane's whole family is part of a search team. Shane and I go out into the woods and hide and wait for the dogs to find us. When they do it's up to us to make sure the dog gets a big reward. Some of them like to be fed liver and others like to play tug-of-war. We have to know what makes the dog that finds us happy and do it the instant they alert."

"What's an alert?"

Gabe's muscles relaxed, that was something he could explain in his sleep.

"When the dog finds someone they have to give a clear indication to the handler. Some dogs bark and stay with the subject, some dogs go back and lead the handler to the subject. That's the alert."

The three men looked at each other and nodded. The bald man looked back at a Gabe. "Tell us about your project."

"Well. The church where my troop meets is more than just a church. Community groups hold bake sales and bike rodeos and lots of activities in the parking lot. A big problem is a lack of available electricity. Power to run stuff comes from the church garage but it only has one light bulb and an outlet. My project is to run power out to the garage from the church, install a breaker panel and run circuits for extension cords and lighting."

"Who is the primary benefactor of this project? You know it can't be the troop, don't you?"

"Yes sir. I know. The troop does hold a rummage sale in the parking lot but I made a list of groups that use the lot and the troop has only ten percent of the activities." Gabe passed the list to the men and the colored pie chart which showed who used the lot.

"I'm a little concerned this project is beyond the skill level of most scouts. How are you going to get participation for the other scouts?" the bald man asked.

"I thought about it. I'm going to work with the adult leader for the electricity merit badge. I'll help him and we'll teach the badge to the scouts. As long as they are putting in the conduit and boxes they aren't in any danger. And it's the bulk of the work."

"All right, but how are you going to be sure the lines are done correctly? You don't want to cause a fire," the man leading the meeting asked.

"One of our adult leaders, Mr. Povlovski, is a licensed electrician. He's going to watch what we're doing and make sure nothing like that will happen. Several of the dads in the Troop are familiar with doing wiring. They'll be following my plan and do the actual wiring."

"How do you intend to make the plan?"

"I've researched the code requirements and then used the Electrician's Handbook to size the wire and make sure it can handle the resistance and heat to be safe." Gabe handed over copies of pages from the books he'd used.

"Where are the materials coming from? You do realize that you can't buy the materials yourself?"

Gabe flipped some pages in his project book. He placed it flat on the table. "This page is the list of the materials." He pointed to the page to the right.

"This page lists the local electrical supply houses and what each of them is willing to donate for the project. Everything on the list is promised."

The men exchanged glances again. The bald man smiled and looked back at Gabe.

"Give us a minute, son."

Gabe leaned back in the chair and watched the men. They spoke in low voices and then wrote some things down on their papers.

"All right Scout Turner. It looks like you have made a concerted plan and have a project that is possible to perform, serves the community and will increase the skill level of the boys in your troop. Your project is approved and we look forward to the presentation of your completed project report."

All the men stood and Gabe scrambled to his feet. Each man shook his hand and smiled at him. The bald man escorted him out to his Dad.

*****

Gabe watched the scouts as they worked inside the garage.

"Okay, Rob, now that you've measured twice, circle the mark you made on the conduit." Gabe pointed to the place on the silver metal tube the scout held. "Good. Now make your cut."

Gabe stepped back and watched the boy wielding a pipe cutter. Shane came over and handed Gabe a glass of icy water. It was May first and the temperature had already been in the eighties for three straight days.

"Hydrate or die." Shane said. Gabe took a long pull on the straw and adjusted the bandanna keeping the sweat out of his eyes.

"How long do you think this is going to take?" Shane asked.

"Actually it's going pretty well. Even with the heat we're almost two days ahead of schedule." Gabe looked up to see a scout climbing into a car. He shoved the glass into Shane's hands and sprinted to the vehicle.

"Hey, Tommy, you forgot to check out." Gabe looked at the driver and recognized the scout's mother. "Hi, Mrs. Howell."

"Sorry."

"No big deal. I just need to know how many hours people worked on my project and I need to be sure you leave with a parent."

"I wish I didn't have to bail on you," Tommy said, "I have to get my braces adjusted."

"Been there, so I know better than to tell you to have fun." Gabe collected the clipboard from the scout and stepped back from the car. He looked back at the garage. Two more hours and they would have all the conduit and boxes up. Then the dads would come in to pull wire. This time next week and Gabe would have finished the project. He had done it. He was going to make Eagle!

Gabe glanced up at the brilliant blue bowl overhead. "Thanks, God, I needed this," he said.

Gabe walked back to Shane. "So are your parents still up for taking me to church or should I ride my bike?"

Shane grinned. "Sit next to you all sweaty from the bike ride, no way. We'll pick you up like usual." Shane started to walk away and then stopped. "You know, Pastor Allen already sent your recommendation in. You don't have to keep coming to church anymore if you don't want to."

Gabe's stomach turned to ice. How could he admit the service made him relax and feel warm inside? For once Shane's poker face was on. Would he think he was a dork for wanting to come? Here goes nothing.

"Ducking out now would be sort of like lying. It would be like I had just pretended to go to get the recommendation. Besides, I like Pastor Allen's sermons. I learn stuff."

Shane's face seemed to glow and the smile was back in full force. "Yeah. Cool. Just don't let Mom know or she'll embarrass you to death celebrating."

Shane walked away to pass out more water and Gabe moved to check another scout's work.

"Why was I afraid to admit what I feel? I should know by now that Shane is my friend," Gabe said.

CHAPTER 20

Gabe sprawled on his bed and carefully penned in answers to his Eagle project handbook. Why did it seem that he had to look up every third word to make sure it was spelled correctly? The air conditioning vent over head cooled his body and gently moved his papers. The inspector had checked the project inside and out and signed off last night. All that remained was to submit the write up to the Advancement Chairman and then it was out of Gabe's hands until the presentations began.

Sweat made the pen slip. The idea of standing up in front of the Eagle committee and reporting on his work made his hands wet and clammy.

He thought, "I'll be all alone in there. What if I make a mistake?" An icy chill slid from his toes up his body. "Oh yeah, God'll be there, I won't be alone," Gabe thought. The icy chill melted but his arms and legs now felt like lead, weighing at least a ton a piece. He closed his eyes and flopped back against the pillows. Gradually his arms and legs came back to life. He dragged his eyelids open and picked up the pen.

"God's always with me but it's up to me to do my best. The search team will let me practice doing the presentation on them. If I'm prepared and God is with me, I can't lose," Gabe told himself.

"Gabe," his Dad's shout was muffled by the closed door of his room, "Dinner."

Gabe flipped the booklet closed and headed for the kitchen.

"Grab what ever side dishes you want and come on out on the patio." Dad wore Mom's frilly pink apron again. Gabe grabbed a plate and loaded up on potato salad, green salad and snagged up a glass of ice cold milk. He hurried across the living room and out the sliding glass door to the patio. His dad speared a couple of sausages and dropped them on Gabe's plate. Settling into the cool metal chair he plopped his plate on the table and closed his eyes to recite a mental Grace.

The table rocked as he Amen'd. His dad had settled in across from him.

"How's the write up going?"

"Pretty good. I'm almost done and Mr. O'Hara said he'd check it before I turn it in."

"Do I need to run it up there?"

"Nope. Shane's going to meet me at the ice cream stand over on Main Street tomorrow after school. He'll take it home to his Dad."

"Don't be too late. It's hard to see cyclists after dark."

"I won't."

His dad put down his fork and knife and focused on Gabe. "I'm proud of you. This hasn't been easy and you've really come up to the challenge."

Can I ask him? Is this the time to see if he'll go to church with me?

"So is now a good time to ask for a - car?"

"I'm a big fat chicken, baulk-baulk baulk," Gabe thought and stayed silent.

His dad laughed, wadded his napkin into a ball and pitched it at Gabe.

Gabe joined the laughter and bent down to pick up the piece of cloth. "Here, you've got sausage juice on your chin." He tossed it back to his Dad.

*****

The bell rang. He hurried out the door and down the hall to the lab room. For the spring semester, Gabe had physics instead of chemistry. He settled himself on the stool at one of the side tables and opened his notebook on the big black rectangular top. Bright sunshine poured in through the windows. Gabe glanced in the opposite direction only to spot Jazz and Daniel at the same bench whispering to each other. He jerked his head around to the front of the class where the teacher stood.

"Good afternoon class," Mr. Higgins said, "We're working on electric circuits today." The teacher began drawing on the white board. "This is a simple circuit diagram with a resistor and single pole switch. You should be able to recognize, and where necessary, draw these symbols." He turned to look at the class.

Gabe copied the drawing into his notebook.

Mr. Higgins turned back to the board and made another drawing. "Can anyone tell me what this is?"

Gabe raised his hand.

"Gabe."

"It's a parallel circuit."

"Very good, but can you tell me which path will carry more current?"

"No sir, I don't know the area or length of the wire so I can't calculate which has a higher resistance."

Gabe had him; it was a trick question.

The teacher stopped and stared at Gabe. "Wire resistance calculations are a little more advanced material than we'll go into here. Are you saying you can calculate the resistance of wire already?"

"Yes sir, I learned how so I could do my Eagle project."

"You're an Eagle Scout?" Mr. Higgins asked.

"Not yet, I have to present my completed project to the committee." He could feel the heat rising in his face as the rest of the class stared. Even Jazz and Daniel were speechless.

Mr. Higgins stepped around the teacher's desk and walk up to Gabe.

"That's close enough for me." He gave Gabe the Scout

salute and reached out to shake his hand. "Welcome to the rank of Eagle."

Gabe returned the salute and hand shake automatically. Mr. Higgins was an Eagle Scout!

Gabe sat back down and Mr. Higgins returned to the front of the room. Daniel scowled at Gabe.

"What's the big deal about this Eagle stuff? You sure Turner isn't a pigeon instead?"

The class laughed. Gabe hid his burning face by pretending to look at his notebook.

Mr. Higgins turned to Daniel. "You'd do well to pay more respect to Gabe. Only four out of a hundred boy scouts ever makes it to the rank of Eagle. It's an accomplishment which will give him entry into some of the best colleges in the country. If he chooses to enter the military it will automatically give him a rank advancement over his fellow recruits."

"Yeah, to head janitor." Daniel winked at Jazz and the whole class laughed again.

"I am well aware of Mr. Turner's position here at the school. If you bothered to stop looking down your nose and talk to the man, you'd find a kind and intelligent individual."

Mr. Higgins picked up the marker and then looked back at Daniel. "What I don't understand is what reason you have to look down on Gabe? He's proven himself to be dedicated and accomplished. What have you done?"

"How do you know I'm not an Eagle Scout?" Daniel's face had turned a dark red.

"Your actions, Daniel, they give you away. Nothing you do demonstrates the ideals or goals of scouting. I know Gabe will make something good of himself. From what I've heard from your other teachers, what you'll make of yourself remains to be seen."

Silence. Gabe could hear the air coming from the vent next to him. Wow, what next?

Mr. Higgins returned to the board and drew another circuit. Gradually the sounds of pages turning and the scratch of pens returned.

*****

Gabe balanced his science book on his lunch tray and looked around the crowded cafeteria for a place to sit. Spying an open spot off to the left, he turned quickly. The tray flew out of his hands and over his shoulder. If he hadn't turned he'd have worn mustard again. "Daniel, this is getting really old. You can stop anytime."

"Yeah, make me, Turner." Daniel disappeared into the crowd.

Gabe fished his book out of the mess on the floor. Finding a dry napkin he wiped off the chili sauce and set it aside while he cleaned up the wasted pile of food.

"God, please forgive me if it's wrong, but, I'm getting Shane to teach me how to stop this tonight," he promised.

CHAPTER 21

Shane tucked Gabe's presentation booklet into the large pocket of his pack. Gabe's stomach flip-flopped watching it go. Maybe some ice cream would help.

He stepped up to the window, and a girl about his age with straight brown hair, wearing a white paper hat, slid the screen up.

"Can I help you?"

"Yeah, I'll have a banana split and," Gabe turned to Shane, "What are you having?"

"A small chocolate shake," Shane said.

The girl wrote the order on a piece of paper and closed the screen.

"I can pay for my shake."

"No problem, I 've still got my snow shoveling money."

"You should save it so you can buy a car."

"All I have is a learner's permit. It's a little early to be looking at cars."

The girl slid the screen open and passed out their order. He handed some bills across and pocketed the coins she returned. Shane tossed a dollar into the cup marked "tips" and walked over to a red metal bench. Gabe spooned up a mouthful of warm chocolate sauce and crushed pineapple and then followed Shane.

He swallowed. "Do you remember the camp out where Chuck tried to shove you into the oatmeal?"

Shane crossed his eyes and sucked on his straw. "I don't think I'll ever forget it. Why?"

"I wondered if you could teach me some bouncer moves."

Shane made some loud gurgling noises as he moved the straw around the bottom of the empty paper cup.

"Yeah. I can, but I can tell you from experience, it's no fun to have to use them and they only work on defense."

Gabe scrapped the last of the caramel syrup and peanuts from the bottom of his dish. "What do you mean?"

"It uses the force of the person's attack. If they swing real hard, you'll throw them a long way." Shane dropped his cup into the trash receptacle.

"What if someone is hitting something you're carrying?"

"Okay, what's going on? Who's giving you a hard time?"

Gabe dropped his bowl in to the trash. "Just a kid at school. He keeps flipping my lunch tray and dumping my food down the front of me."

Shane grabbed a tray sitting next to the window and walked back over to Gabe. "Pretend I'm you, what does he do?"

Gabe slapped the front of the tray, tipping it toward Shane. Shane sat on the bench and looked at the tray. "Okay I think I've got it." He switched his grip. "Try it again."

Gabe punched the tray harder. Shane stepped in really close and the tray flipped toward Gabe.

"How did you do that?" Gabe asked.

"Grip the front corners and rest the back corners on your forearms. When the kid reaches out to hit the tray, step into him. He'll end up wearing your lunch instead." Shane handed the tray to Gabe. "You try it."

Holding the tray felt awkward. As Shane reached out Gabe stepped in very carefully. The tray came up too slow.

"You've got to move in faster."

"I don't want to step on your foot."

"I've had horses step on me so you're not going to hurt me. Remember, I'm this jerk giving you a hard time. He deserves a little foot stomping."

"Is that what Jesus would say?"

"Probably not, so don't go out to stomp him, but don't worry about protecting him either."

Gabe grasped the tray again. When Shane reached out, he stepped in and let his arms drop. The tray flipped up and hit Shane's nose.

"Oh man, I'm sorry." Gabe dropped the tray and reached for Shane's face.

He laughed and stepped back. "Don't worry, it's not even bleeding. I think you got it."

Gabe picked up the tray and put it back by the window.

"You know it won't end there." Shane said.

"What won't?"

"The whole spilling your lunch thing." Shane walked back to the bench. "If this kid is the kind of weasel to spill your lunch for the fun of it, he's going to scream bloody murder when it backfires."

"What should I do, skip eating?" Gabe sat down. "I'm almost doing it now. I guess it would save my lunch money."

"No way. Just be ready for the next step." Shane smiled. "I could be wrong but he's either going to make a big fuss and say you did it deliberately or he's going to try and sucker punch you."

"Should I lie? I'm no good at it." Gabe used his sleeve to wipe sweat off his forehead.

"Lying is wrong. Just make a big deal about being so sorry for dumping the food on him and apologizing for being a klutz. Since your tray has gone flying before, a lot people will believe you and he either has to keep quiet or own up to knocking your tray around."

"What if he tries to punch me?"

"Hold your tray so it covers your stomach and stay jammed really close to him so he can't swing. If he does try and punch it will hit the tray or be obvious and he'll get suspended."

Gabe rested his elbows on his knees and his chin on his hands.

"Can you think of any other way to do this?"

"Brown bag or skip lunch."

"That's the coward's way out, isn't it?"

"No it's a form of turning the other cheek but from the sounds of things it won't stop this kid. He's getting his jollies bullying you."

"I just don't get it. I'm bigger and stronger than him. If I sat on him he'd break in half. Why won't he leave me alone?"

"Mom calls it a Napoleon complex. It makes him feel important to push bigger kids around."

"Ever had to deal with being tripped?" Gabe asked.

"He's tripping you, too?"

Gabe nodded. "If I get called to the board, I have to really watch it or he trips me and the whole class laughs."

"Okay. First avoid the situations, sit in the front row. If you have assigned seats ask to be moved to the front so you can see the board better."

"What about in the cafeteria?"

"You know you're going to go down anyway. Dump your lunch on him."

"Great so I'm still a clown."

"Practice walking where you keep your shoulders and hips over your feet. You may have to take a shorter stride, but you should be able to catch yourself instead of going down."

Gabe stood and started to walk over to his bike. "Thanks."

"I'm not done yet. You might as well learn it all."

"What do you mean?"

"Sooner or later this kid is going to throw a punch. If you punch back, you're expelled."

"So, what do I do? Let him hit me or run?"

"Neither. You use the force of the punch to get him off his feet. Then you run."

Gabe turned back. "How?"

"Pretend your going to punch me."

No way, he'll kill him. He balled his right hand and swung in slow motion. He should be able to duck this. Shane yanked Gabe's wrist and pushed on his shoulder. His weight shifted forward onto his toes. He tried to windmill his arms but the right one continued to pull him forward. Oh, man, I'm going down. Shane switched his grip and pulled him back up.

Shane panted. "Of course you wouldn't stop his fall and its easier if the guy swings faster. The nice part is the harder he swings the harder he falls. Now you try."

Gabe rolled his shoulders and stood waiting.

"Widen you stance a little and bend your knees. You've got to be able to move without changing your feet and still keep your balance."

Gabe spread his feet and bent his knees like in baseball. Shane took a swing and Gabe grabbed and pushed. Shane would have ended up in a face plant if Gabe hadn't grabbed his shirt collar and hauled him up. "Whoa, it works."

"There are some other nasties but I promised Dad I wouldn't show them to anyone or use them unless they had a weapon and attacked me." Shane walked back over to the bench and sat down.

"You can do worse then giving someone a street pizza face?"

"Deliberately breaking bones is the next step."

His stomach tried to push the banana split back up. "How does your dad know all this?"

"You remember the old movie Roadhouse?"

Gabe nodded up and down.

"My dad worked in one to pay for college."

"So when it comes to a fight, I want your dad on my side?"

"Yup."

"Anything else I should know?"

"What to do if he grabs your shirt. Hold his hands in place so he can't get away and lean forward and down. He has to hit the ground." Shane demonstrated. "Or grab his thumb and peel it back away from you. He has to let go, but watch for a punch to come from the other hand."

Gabe sat back down on the bench. "All of this kind of bothers me. I mean, is it the Christian thing to do?"

"I honestly don't know. I don't think God meant for Christians to be punching bags, but I could be wrong. All I know is I don't start it, I try and walk away and when none of that works I use what the other guy throws to protect myself. If he leaves me alone, nothing happens."

"I guess I've got to think about this and decide if I can do it." He got up and walked over to his bike. Shane followed a step behind him.

Shane climbed on his mountain bike and grabbed the handle bars. "Just remember, once you start, you can't quit and he's going to get a lot meaner until he realizes he can't win."

He popped a wheelie and rode off toward home.

CHAPTER 22

Gabe shifted his grip on the insulated fabric lunch bag and hurried across the cafeteria. The line for hot lunches already snaked out the big double doors and he could see students rushing for a place at the end. He was glad not to be in that congestion.

Craning his neck, he spotted an open table bathed in sunshine in the outside eating area and headed for it. He turned sideways to slip by a couple having an argument in the doorway to the patio. A crash behind him and shouts of "fight" stopped him. Looking over at the commotion he saw Daniel and Eric Long pushing each other. Food smeared the front of Eric's shirt and pants. Monitors converged on the boys and pulled them apart.

Gabe's first reaction turned him toward the melee. He took one step and then stopped. He couldn't do anything to help. He didn't see anything. Just because he knew Daniel deliberately spilled Eric's food, didn't mean he could prove anything,

He turned back toward his table. He slid into the seat just before another boy took it.

Whew!

"You can sit here, too." Gabe waved to an open chair. The white metal table had four seats bolted to the base.

"Thanks but we've got four and there are only three places left."

Gabe looked around. The other tables filled rapidly with groups of people. He wished he had friends to sit with. It'd be nice if Shane went to this school. He unzipped the green pouch and unloaded two sandwiches, a soda, some carrots sticks and a package of Ho Ho's. Brown bagging lunch has its advantages. He could have soda and junk food and have more than five minutes to eat.

The cold tuna salad inside the soft bread practically melted in his mouth. He finished the first sandwich in four big bites. He paused to drink soda, letting the fizz play on his tongue. He unwrapped the second sandwich.

"Okay if we sit with you? The other tables are full."

Gabe recognized one boy from his physics class, but not the other one. "Yeah, sure."

The boys dropped their trays on the table and twisted the chairs so they could sit down.

"You're Gabe, aren't you?"

"That's me. I think we have physics together."

"Yup, I'm Angelo, I hide in the back of the class." He jerked a thumb at the other boy. "This is Tom."

Gabe extended his hand. "Hi."

Tom stopped eating long enough to shake hands.

"Did you hear what happened to Eric Long?" Angelo asked.

"No I saw him mixing it up with Daniel. I figured Daniel knocked his tray over, but I didn't see what happened."

"You and me both; that's Case's favorite pass time."

Angelo chewed another mouthful and swallowed. "Now Eric's been suspended for three days for fighting."

Gabe choked on his soda. "If they suspended him, what'd they do to Daniel?"

"Nothing. His Dad's some big wig and the administration is scared he'll have them fired or something."

"That's just wrong." Gabe paused with his last bite of cake in his hand.

"Welcome to Indian Creek School, where you ain't right unless your parents are important and then you're never wrong."

The bell rang ending lunch. Gabe folded his bag and stuffed it into his pack. Angelo and Tom hurried toward the tray line while Gabe headed for the exit. He tossed his trash in the can by the door and headed down the hall.

So he had made the right decision to avoid a conflict. Maybe Shane and my dad were right. Avoiding trouble was the right path.

*****

"Hey Mom, where's the bread?" Gabe closed the cupboard and turned to face her.

"Sorry honey, we're out."

"What should I make for lunch?" No way, this is the last full day of school.He couldn't have brown bagged it all this time for nothing.

"I really don't have anything. I wanted to use up the food before we went camping tomorrow. Can't you buy something?"

"I guess so." Gabe turned away and hurried to his room. It's only one day. He could skip lunch.

*****

Gabe sat in math class and listened to Mr. Nelson talk about geometry. A smile curled his lips knowing he'd be in the regular math class next fall and not dummy math. His stomach growled. The girl sitting next to him turned quickly, with a startled expression on her face.

Heat climbed his neck and cheeks. Great. Why did they have to take the vending machines out of the lobby? He could have gotten a candy bar or some chips to make it through the day. His stomach rumbled again only louder. The girl glanced over and giggled.

The bell rang ending class. Gabe swung his backpack on his back and headed for the cafeteria. He stopped just outside the wooden doors and made sure both pack straps were on his shoulders and his hands were free.

Here goes.

He pushed the door open and stepped into line. The lunch lady looked up and gave him a big smile. "Long time no see hon.; you been skipping lunch?"

"No, I have more time to eat if I bring lunch."

"Makes sense." She adjusted the hair net knot. "The usual?"

"Yup."

Gabe lowered the paper plate to his tray, collected three cartons of chocolate milk and scanned his ID. He looked around and spotted an empty seat before picking up his tray. He walked carefully, taking small steps and trying to avoid people. One table short of his destination, Daniel jumped to his feet and reached for the bottom of the tray.

He asked for it. Gabe stepped in and dropped his hands as he heard a pop from the bottom of his tray. A chili coated hotdog rolled down the front of Daniel's shirt, leaving a rust colored path in its wake. Onions landed in a small pile on his toes and mustard streaked his shorts. Daniel really shouldn't have worn flip flops.

Gabe leaned in and whispered in Daniel's ear.

"Free ride's over. Whatever you do to me is going to turn and come back on you. Leave me alone and I leave you alone. This is your only warning."

He stood up straight and raised his voice so everyone around him could hear. "Oh I'm so sorry. I'm such a klutz. I've spilled so many lunches this year. Maybe next year you should stay further away from me so this doesn't happen again."

Daniel's face turned an ugly red. "I intended this for Long, but you deserve it just as much, Turner."

Gabe felt something drive the tray into him. He looked down to see Daniel's fist against the plastic surface and something white in his hand.

"I saw that, young man, your coming with me to the Dean's office." The monitor rushed up to them.

Gabe felt a chill run up his spine. After all this, was he caught?

The monitor reached out and grabbed Daniel's collar. "I don't know what your problem is but I saw you try and punch this boy. Thank goodness the tray was in the way." He grabbed Daniel's wrist with his other hand and pulled it into view. As he did Daniel opened his hand letting something fall to the ground.

"What was that?" The monitor's eyes opened wider.

Gabe stepped back and looked down. A plastic knife, chipped down to a sharp point, and sometimes called a shiv, lay at his feet. He looked up at the monitor. A wave of dizziness circled his head.

If he hadn't been holding the tray like Shane warned, he would have been stabbed.

Two more monitors converged on them. The one holding Daniel turned to the others. "Pick up that knife this boy just dropped and get the big one's information, then bring him to the Dean's office. This one's getting expelled."

Numbness climbed his legs and made his knees go weak. Shane's words came back to him,

"If this kid is the kind of weasel to spill your lunch for the fun of it, he's going to scream bloody murder when it backfires."

One of the monitors grabbed his arm. Jazz jumped up tears running down her face and collected her tray.

"I hate you Turner. I'll never see Daniel again because of you."

She dumped her tray and ran into the washroom.

Gabe's gaze took in her retreat. How could he have ever thought that he was in love with her?

The monitor watched her go with an incredulous expression on his face. He shook his head and turned back to Gabe. "Let's go, son."

If I come up against Daniel alone, no one's going to back me. Angelo's right, it's all about having your parents around when you get hauled in front of the administration. Dad may not be important, but I'll have better chance with him there then not.

"Look, I don't feel so good, could we stop by the nurse on the way to the Dean's, please?"

"You look pretty pale," the man nodded. He held Gabe's arm all the way to the nurse's office.

Gabe wondered if the monitor thought that he was going to escape.

Pushing the door open with his shoulder, he spoke to the blonde lady in the white nurse's uniform. "Julie, call this boy's parents. He may be headed into shock."

She jumped from behind her desk and guided Gabe to the cot. She had him lie down and put a rolled up blanket under his feet. She covered him with a second blanket and tucked it in around him and gently removed his student id lanyard from around his neck. "You doing okay? Is your stomach upset?"

"A little. Can you call my Dad?"

"Rest. He'll be here in no time."

Gabe watched her walk over to the computer and heard keys clicking. He heard her speaking into the telephone.

"Mr. Turner. Oh it's you Rich, I didn't put the names together. Your son has been in a fracas in the lunch room. They were taking him to the Dean's office but he said he didn't feel well and they brought him here. He asked to have us call you."

She paused.

"He's not hurt, just upset. I'm keeping an eye on him." Another shorter pause and then she hung up.

Gabe closed his eyes, the scene replaying in his head. He heard the door open and saw his dad come through the portal. Gabe started to sit up and felt his Dad's arm slip behind him and help. The worried expression his dad wore was too much. He tried to smile. "Sorry to cause a ruckus. I guess I just needed lunch more than I thought."

He swung his feet to the floor and took a deep breath. Dad held his arm gently and looked ready to catch him if he fell.

"What happened?"

"I think you need to talk to Mr. Gleason about that. As a matter of fact he'd like to talk to your son, too." The nurse said.

His dad came to his feet and whirled around to face her. "I don't give a rat's tail what Gleason wants. I'm taking my son to the emergency room to be checked out and if they release him I'm taking him home."

His dad turned back to him and reached out his hand. "Come on Gabe, the truck's out front."

Gabe pushed away from the cot and stood straight up. Another wave of dizziness made his head spin but settled after a few seconds.

When they got outside, his dad maneuvered him close to the handrail. "Can you manage the steps?"

"Sure." There sat his Dad's truck, up against the curb, driver's door open and the engine rumbling. "You left the truck running?"

"Guess I did." His dad opened the passenger door and Gabe sat on the seat and then swung his legs in. He grabbed the seatbelt and buckled it while his dad closed the door.

"I'm okay Dad, I just need something to eat."

"We'll let a doctor decide that."

"If we go to the emergency room, Mom'll be upset. I don't want her to worry. I wasn't feeling that bad but, I didn't want to face Mr. Gleason without you."

"Gleason is something of a brown-nose and I don't much care for the man, but why should he come down on you?" His dad shifted into gear and pulled out.

"This happened to another guy and he got suspended while Daniel got off. Daniel's dad is somebody important."

"And Gleason's trying to impress him by giving his son special treatment?" His dad pulled out into traffic.

Gabe nodded.

"Who threw the first punch?"

"Nobody. Daniel deliberately tried to spill my tray but ended up wearing the food. Then he tried to stick a sharp pointy thing in my stomach, but the tray was in the way."

His Dad's head snapped around to look at him. "Are you sure you're okay?"

"Fine. Watch out! You're going to rear-end that guy."

His dad slammed on the brakes. The car in front moved out and he still sat there.

"Dad?"

His dad looked back at the road and started to drive again. "Now we're definitely going to the ER."

"Why?"

"A little bit of gamesmanship. We need to go on record this boy came after you with a weapon, makes it harder for the administration to bury the incident. And if Mom gets home and you haven't been to the doctor we'll both be in a lot of trouble with her. You know the house rule."

"Don't mess with the person who cooks your food or could starch your underwear?"

"You got it."

CHAPTER 23

Great, first day of summer vacation and where was he? In the dean's office. Gabe tightened his grip on the wooden handles of the chair and he pressed down with his heels. Every time he let up the pressure, his foot bounced up and down creating an annoying tapping.

His dad sat in the chair next to him. "Don't worry, this won't take long. We'll be on the road to Wisconsin in no time."

"I hope Mom's okay in the car. It's awfully hot."

"She has the keys and can run the air and she has a new novel. She'll probably tell us to get lost so she can finish one more chapter when we come out."

"Sorry to keep you waiting." Mr. Gleason hurried in and sat behind his desk.

"I've heard Daniel's side of this and now I'd like to hear yours, ah"- he consulted a piece of paper-"Gabriel."

"All year long Daniel's been making a point of knocking my tray out of my hands. Some times his buddies would push me at the same time. I'd end up covered in food and my clothes stained and all the kids get a big laugh."

"But you never reported it." Mr. Gleason rested his elbows on the chair arms and pressed his fingers together.

"I did once but Daniel's buddies said it wasn't true. The monitor told me I'd get detention if I tried to cause trouble again."

Gabe shifted in his chair.

His dad wasn't smiling anymore.

"I tried avoiding him but at least once a week, they'd hassle me and spill my lunch. Finally, I started brown bagging it."

"Then why did you buy lunch on Thursday?" Mr. Gleason leaned forward.

"I didn't get a chance to make one so I had to buy."

"Daniel was quite upset that you spilled your lunch on him. Did you do it intentionally?"

Gabe sat forward in his chair. "No."

"Then why was the food all over Daniel and none on you? He says you started the fight by deliberately dumping your tray on him. The evidence seems to support his claims."

His arms started shaking. He swallowed the lump and tried to talk in a normal voice.

"I was really tired of having my clothes ruined so Daniel could make his buddies laugh. I carried the tray differently, holding the front corners instead of the sides. If no one touched the tray everything would be fine, but if someone hit it like Daniel had been doing, they would end up wearing the food instead of me." Gabe swallowed another lump. "If he had left me alone, nothing would have happened."

"So you tried to take matters into your own hands."

"It doesn't sound like he had any alternative," Dad said.

Mr. Gleason gave his dad a cold stare, "There are always alternatives, but we're getting off track." The Dean turned back to Gabe. "So what happened next?"

"When I walked by, Daniel stood up and smacked my tray and all the food spilled on him. I felt something hit the tray and I thought he'd tried to punch me, but when the monitor grabbed his hand he had a sharp thing in it."

Mr. Gleason picked up a sealed plastic bag with writing on it and handed it to Gabe. "Is this it?"

He reached across the desk and took the package. "It looks like it." His hand started to shake so he dropped it onto the desk and grabbed the chair arms again.

"I think I've heard enough." Mr. Gleason picked up the papers on his desk and scanned them for a moment, then turned back to Gabe. "Under the circumstances, I won't suspend you for provoking a fight. However, I will have the Para pros watch you closely next term and if there is any more trouble you will either be suspended or expelled. I won't allow troublemakers in my school."

"What?" Gabe and his dad said at the same time.

"You won't allow troublemakers in your school? What about the boy that's been bullying my son for an entire year?" His dad sat on the edge of his seat.

"So your son says. I don't have any proof other than his word." Mr. Gleason smiled at Dad.

"My son did nothing and was attacked by a student with a shiv. It was just sheer luck he wasn't injured. I want to know what you're doing to punish the other boy and prevent this from happening again."

"That is none of your business. It is between the administration and the other boy's family."

The muscle in Dad's jaw twitched. "If you don't give me an answer, considering the tenor of this conversation, I will have to assume you are not punishing the boy who attempted to injure my son. That is a clear violation of school policy. If you are making special rules for certain students, then I'll be left with no alternative other than to sue for discrimination."

"I shouldn't tell you this, but since you are a school employee, I'll bend the rules, just this once. He will be given a suspension at the start of the next school year and he's been told to avoid Gabriel as much as possible." Mr. Gleason put his papers down and stood up. "Now, if you have any other questions, you'll have to make another appointment when you aren't so emotional."

"This is far from settled and I'm not going anywhere until it is." Dad sat back in his chair and stretched his legs out in front of him. "Let's start with the student handbook. Having a weapon on school property is grounds for expulsion, but you're giving this other kid special treatment and I want to know why?"

"I've made my decision, Mr. Turner. Your belligerent attitude will not change anything, but it does give me an understanding of where your son gets his poor social skills from."

Mr. Gleason's face had paled and his hands were shaking.

"It looks like I'll have to take this in front of the school board."

Mr. Gleason smirked, "Go right ahead. They'll probably expel your son instead of giving him a warning."

Dad narrowed his eyes and stared at the Dean. "The other boy is named Case, isn't he? Is he any relation to John Case, the school board president?"

"Daniel is John's son. The boy has excellent potential to get into a good college. Of course his father isn't going to stand for an expulsion on his record ruining those chances. There is no way you will win."

His dad stood up and motioned to Gabe to come along. "If he thinks expulsion will hurt the kid's college chances, wait until he sees what a stint in Juvenile Hall does to his record."

Mr. Gleason hurried to block their path. "Wait. What are you going to do?"

"We're going down the street to the police station and file assault charges."

"But wait, you can't do that. If this gets out the press will destroy us."

"You're willing to leave a violent student in the school to mollify someone you think has political clout. I'm banking on the press causing so much trouble you lose your job and Case has to resign from the scandal. You don't belong in this position and if this is an example of his actions he doesn't belong in his."

Dad reached for the door handle.

"Please don't do that, I'm sure we can work something out."

"If the student is permanently expelled from the Indian Creek System by the time we get back from our vacation, we'll drop the charges. If not, we go to the press. Your choice."

Gabe walked out the door. His father started to follow and then stopped.

"You'd best hang onto that weapon. I'm sure the police will take matters into their own hands if it disappears. I'm sure they have the report we made at the ER by now."

He closed the door and led the way back to the car.

CHAPTER 24

"It feels good to get back into the swing of scouting." Gabe stretched his arms up over his head. "Having my mom along camping for two weeks felt strange." Gabe liked the tent at the top of the hill. It was a little removed from the other boys. When ever they came to scout camp, he would rush to stake his claim.

"I hear you. If I hadn't had my iPod I'd have been bored to tears visiting all the relatives back East. The whole summer has been wasted." Shane sat next to the campfire in front of their tent. "I still can't believe your dad took on the Dean. I mean he's always so easy going." Sharing it with Shane had been easy. They'd cleared the ground and dug a fire-pit. After lining it with stones, they'd started a roaring fire and were able to just hang out. Unless he stood up and looked to the south, it felt like he was all alone.

"I've never seen him act that way. He was more like himself at the police station." Gabe took a sip of his Mountain Dew. "He works part-time with the fire department as a paramedic so the desk sergeant knew him. We filled out some paperwork and I had to swear what I'd said was true. The sergeant called on the radio for someone to go get the stuff from Mr. Gleason and to go to Daniel's house."

"What happened then?"

"We got in the car and went camping."

"You're joking." Shane said.

"Nope. By the time we got back, Daniel had been transferred to Holy Cross and we had a letter from the superintendent promising he wouldn't be back to Indian Creek. His dad has announced he won't run for school board president again."

Shane sipped his Dew. "I'm really sorry I got you into trouble. I guess I shouldn't have showed you that stuff."

Gabe tried to look Shane in the eyes but the kid had his head tipped down and wouldn't look up.

"Hey, you didn't get me in trouble. I think you saved my life."

Shane looked up. "How?"

"Daniel had that knife thing in his hand when he stood up. If things had gone as usual, my belly would have been wide open to him and I'd have been so busy trying to clean up, I never would have seen it coming." He saw Shane let out his breath and rub his eyes.

"I'm really glad it's over." Shane said.

"So am I."

Gabe stood up, grabbed a log and placed it in the center of the coals. Within seconds the bark caught and the sap flared up, exploding with loud pops and hisses.

"So how did your Eagle presentation go?"

"It was pretty much the same as the project proposal only I showed pictures of the work getting done and had to show how many hours and what materials were donated."

He leaned way over and grabbed the jar of cookies they shared. He unscrewed the top, snagged a couple and passed the jar to Shane. "I can't believe your mom made enough cookies for the whole troop."

"It's the first time we made a full recipe of Monster cookies. It took a dozen eggs and three pounds of brown sugar, a bag of chocolate chips and a bag of M&M's. You should have seen the huge box of oatmeal we used, and that was a single batch." He pulled out his own treat and screwed the lid back on. "I still can't believe she kept a straight face when she told Mr. C. they weren't fattening because they didn't have flour."

Gabe laughed and got cookie crumbs down his windpipe. He sat up and coughed to clear his throat.

"Now that your project's approved, when is your Court of Honor?"

"It'll be after school starts. National needs time to review everything. I want you to be one of the scouts who lights candles for the story of the scouting path to Eagle."

"What do I have to do?"

"Mrs. Whitmore will read a section for each rank. When she reads the one for your rank, you go up and light a candle next to that emblem."

"I can do that, but I better get my rear end over to Trailblazers the rest of this week. I want to make First Class before we go home, I've got four more days. I can do it." Shane tossed sticks into the flames. "So what do you want as a present?"

"My parents to come to church." Gabe picked up a stick and started drawing designs in the dirt.

"Have you asked them?"

"No, I don't know why but every time I try the words stick in my throat. I don't think Dad likes the idea of religion, but I don't know why. I guess I'm a big chicken."

"I wouldn't want to ask my dad to do something he didn't believe in."

"Yeah, but your dad knows how to kill people. It pays to be careful with him."

Shane laughed, "You better hope he's not sneaking up the path."

Gabe spun around, his heart pounding. The empty path greeted him. Shane laughed.

"Funny guy. Watch out, I'm going to sit on you."

"Okay, I give up."

Gabe moved back to his stump chair and attempted to control his laughter. Shane's contagious giggles erupted occasionally and made him snicker.

"I can't believe school starts in a couple of weeks."

Shane made a face. "Don't remind me. What are you taking?"

"That's another thing I want to talk to Dad about. I liked

my project and the calculations clicked. I didn't have to think about it and be afraid I had made a mistake."

"So how does this involve your dad and school?"

"I think I've made up my mind to become an electrician, but that means switching my schedule around so I can go to the tech campus and take electrical courses." Gabe tossed his stick into the flames.

"Why would that bother your Dad?" Shane asked.

"I wouldn't take the courses needed to go to college. When I get out of high school, I'd go into an apprentice program and start work."

"And your dad wants you to go to college."

"I think so. He's always said he wanted me to have the education he couldn't afford."

"Which one do you think is going to upset him more?"

"I'm not sure, but I think the going to church."

"If it was me, I'd start with the easy question and see how he reacted and then ask the tough one."

"What do you do if they're both tough?"

"Pray hard for guidance and then follow your heart."

"Does that work?"

"I don't know I haven't come up against it with my parents yet."

"Keep this up and I'm going to duct tape you to a tree and stuff cookies in your pockets for the bears and raccoons."

Gabe reached for a roll of the silver stuff they had hung from a convenient branch.

"You wouldn't waste the cookies."

Gabe laughed and pretended to reach for Shane. Shane dove to the far side of the fire acting like he believed him. Gabe rolled back into place against the stump.

So God, how do I talk to my Dad? The going to church thing I know you go along with, but is it okay for me to be an electrician?

*****

Gabe walked down the hill and approached the table.

"Okay God, I've been praying for three straight nights. Be with me now." A Coleman lantern hissed as the gas burned with a painfully bright light. The Order of the Arrow ceremony had ended and most of the scouts and leaders quietly read in their tents or packed to go home tomorrow. His dad and Mr. O'Hara sat at the table sipping diet cokes and eating cookies. He could hear the murmur of their voices but not the words. "Hey, Dad?"

Both men looked around and smiled at him. His dad waved him forward. "How're you doing? Are you packed?"

"Yep, all done." He tried to say more but his throat clogged up.

"What's up?" Dad asked.

He sat down on the bench beside Mr. O'Hara and across from his Dad. "I wanted to talk to you about school."

His dad got a serious expression. "Are you worried about some of Daniel's friends trying to bully you?"

"I hadn't even thought about that. I was thinking about my Eagle Project and my future."

"There is life after becoming an Eagle you know." His dad smiled and sipped his soda.

"Yeah, well, the project made me realize just how much fun doing wiring really is. The diagrams, the calculation, looking up the codes, it all seemed so…" he paused what's the right word? "…natural. I don't think I'd do really well in college with the theory stuff but I do think I could be a really good electrician."

He wiped his sweat damp palms on his shorts. He said to himself, "Okay God, it's up to you now. If he says no, I'll figure it's not the path You want for me."

His dad looked down at the table and drank his soda without saying a word. Eons crawled by and then he smiled.

"I think you've really hit on something there. You've got to finish high school though, no dropping out to go to work."

"Oh no, I wasn't even thinking about it. I want to enroll in Tech. I can finish my high school classes for half a day and go get training on doing wiring and layouts the other half and its part of the school program so they run buses and everything."

Mr. O'Hara smiled. "I think you have great idea. Why don't you try Tech campus for a while and if you still like the idea of being an electrician, I'll introduce you to the head of the Union. You need your diploma to get into the apprentice program, but union electricians make a really decent salary and work all year round."

"Do we have to change anything at the school to do this?" Dad asked.

"I'll have to go in and re-arrange my schedule. I can do it the first day, but I'd rather have it set and ready." A smile stretched his face until it almost hurt. He stood up to leave. "Thanks Dad."

He almost skipped up the path to his tent.

"Thank you, thank you, thank you, God. There is a place for me in this world."

Shane sat by the fire feeding the last of the logs they'd gathered. He looked up at the path the question in his eyes.

Gabe came up the last few steps dancing. "He said yes. He liked it. I worried over nothing."

"Yes!" Shane pumped a fist into the air, "Maybe asking them to come to church will be just as easy."

The lightness drained down Gabe's body and he slumped onto his stump. "I hope so."

"When are you going to ask him?" Shane asked.

"When they ask me what I want for my Eagle present." Gabe swallowed hard and then thought,

"Oh man, God, can you make it just as easy?"

CHAPTER 25

Gabe put one empty trash can into the other and carried both up the driveway. He positioned both beside the house and snapped lids into place. Pee-yew, he was glad lunch was two hours behind him and dinner wasn't for a while. He dragged the lawn mower out of the garage, adjusted the choke and throttle and yanked on the starter rope. It roared to life on the second try.

It took an hour to finish both the front and back yards. He shoved the lawn mower back into its spot in the garage and looked at the flower beds. Yuck. Now he'd have to weed. He sank to his knees and grabbed some Creeping Charlie. He wished he could pretend he didn't know a flower from a weed and get out of gardening duty. His next handful included a sticker bush.

"Ouch." He dropped the plants to the ground and stuck his finger in his mouth.

"If you're that hungry, I'm sure we have something in the refrigerator." His Dad laughed. He'd come up the walk behind Gabe.

Gabe grinned back and pulled his finger out of his mouth. "Why do I always leave the job I hate most for last?"

"The eternal hope you'll be rescued?" His dad shifted his jacket to his other hand. "How much more do you have to do?"

"Not much. I mixed up the hamburger with parmesan and

egg and bread crumbs and made some iced tea." Gabe reached out to pull another weed.

"I'll fire up the grill. Wash your hands before you reach for one of my burgers or expect to pull back a stump." His dad continued up the walk.

Gabe went back to work and practiced whistling to relieve the boredom of the job. Thirty minutes later he put the tools back in the garage and walked into the kitchen to wash his hands. The smells wafting in through the screen door made his mouth water.

"Come and get it before I feed it to the dog."

"We don't have a dog." He hurried out the door and onto the back patio. "Where's Mom?"

"She had to work some overtime. We'll save her dinner." His dad slid the spatula under a burger with a swift thrust and lifted it from the heat.

Gabe grabbed a plate with an open bun and moved it within range. The burger landed perfectly centered on the mound of catsup.

"Head's up."

Gabe snatched up the other plate as the second burger slipped from the spatula and headed for the cement. He caught it just before it hit the ground. It wasn't centered but had made it on the bun. He carried both plates to the table and slid into the metal chair.

"Thank you, Lord for this food. Bless it to our use and us to Your service. Amen."

Dad sat down and picked up a fork full of potato salad. "So have you figured out what you want from Mom and me for an Eagle present?"

His throat closed and he choked on the burger. Eyes watering, he applied his napkin to his mouth and coughed.

Here it goes, God.

"I don't want anything expensive."

"Good because you won't get it."

"I just want you and Mom to come to church with me for

three months when we aren't at search practice or camping."

His dad tossed his fork on to his plate. It bounced twice and hopped off onto the ground. His lips pressed tightly together and a muscle worked in his jaw.

"No. I won't be a hypocrite and waste time with something I don't believe in anymore."

Be with me now God, I'm scared. "Why don't you believe? Mr. C. does and the O'Haras do."

His dad closed his eyes and he looked in pain.

Was he having a heart attack?

He opened them again and tossed the napkin on his plate. "I guess you're old enough to know."

"When you were a two-year-old, I was going to school days and working nights. You mother had finally made it to the day shift. So we need someone to watch you and your six-week old sister."

Gabe stared. "I had a sister?"

Yes. Let me finish, though. We hired a lady some friends used sometimes to watch their kids. She seemed nice and competent and was always reliable."

"It turned out that after we left, she would have relatives drop off their kids here for her to watch. One of the kids had chicken pox.

"About two weeks after she started working you and your sister came down with the pox. The fevers were terrible and you were both in the hospital on IV's. You were older and stronger," His dad stopped and closed his eyes for a second. When he spoke again, his voice was husky. "But your sister was just too little and she died in my arms."

"I had a sister? God why did you take her away?" Gabe screamed silently.

"We had done everything we could and I had prayed like I'd never prayed before, but it wasn't enough, Shellie was gone."

"Your mom and I didn't go to church so we went to a local minister. We were stressed and just wanted to get through it. The minister didn't want to do a funeral service for us unless we became members of his church. We signed up and paid the fee that he called a donation and he did the service." His dad swallowed.

"I couldn't sleep and your mother cried all the time. We went to him and asked how God could do this. Why would He let an innocent baby die? The minister said God knew we were weak in faith and this was His test to help us grow. If our faith had been stronger she would have been okay."

His dad stood up. "That was the last time I went to church." He silently walked inside. Gabe heard his parents' bedroom door close.

Gabe sat for a while with tears streaming down his face. He hadn't known. He made Dad live through all of it again because he couldn't stop pushing. Gabe knew that Dad had a reason but did that stop him? No. Push, push, push.

"God please heal my Dad's heart. I never wanted to hurt him." He stood and wiped his tears away with his arm. He wrapped up his Dad's plate and made up another one for his mom and put both in the refrigerator. He put away the food and washed the utensils, wrote a note and grabbed his cell phone.

"Can you meet me at the ice cream stand?"

"Sure. I'll leave now." Shane said.

Gabe closed the phone and hopped on his bike. Pedaling as hard as he could settled his stomach. Shane was waiting for him at the bike stand.

"What's up?"

Gabe walked over to their bench. "I asked my dad to come to church."

"It went that bad?"

"It was worse than bad." Gabe picked up a handful of gravel and started tossing it at a flattened soda can. "I had a baby sister who died and the minister told Dad it was his fault because he didn't have enough faith."

"What a jerk." Shane stood up, his eyes flashed green. He closed his eyes, took a deep breath, and let it out slowly. "What did you say?"

"Nothing. I just sat there like a bump on a log. I don't know what to do or what to say."

"Come on, it's not that far to the church. Let's go see Pastor Allen."

Gabe grabbed his bike and followed Shane down the sidewalk. They got to the church office but the place was empty.

"I forgot Pastor Allen's on vacation this week." Shane kicked at a pebble on the driveway. "Do you want to talk to my mom?"

"I don't know. I have a feeling Dad's kept all this inside for a reason. What if he doesn't want your parents to know?"

"They're his friends. Maybe they can help him."

"No. I'd better not. I'm not going to go blabbing and make it worse." Gabe squeezed his hand brakes to keep his bike steady.

"What are you going to do?" Shane asked.

"Nothing. I'm going to pretend it never happened and if he asks me what I want again, I'll tell him a jack-knife or something."

"Are you going to stop coming to church?"

"I don't know. I really like it but it probably reminds Dad of what happened. Maybe for his sake I should stay home."

"Maybe for his sake you shouldn't." Shane bunny hopped his bike a foot sideways.

"How can making my dad hurt help him?"

"I don't know the right answer, but I do know that minister was full of horse feathers. If your dad sees you going to church and getting something good out of it, maybe he'll give it a try."

"I don't know. I'll have to think about it." The memory of his Dad's expression pressed against the back of his eyes.

"Don't think. Pray. This isn't one for you or me to handle."

Shane coasted down the church driveway and turn onto the street headed for home.

"Please God, what should I do? I thought I had gotten past making a mess of everything."

Gabe pedaled some laps around the parking lot. School started tomorrow and they had search practice planned for the next Sunday so Gabe had more than a week to figure things out. He turned out of the parking lot and headed for home.

CHAPTER 26

Gabe walked up the shallow steps to the front of the school, his backpack slung over his shoulder as usual. Jazz stood in a cluster of girls off to one side talking to a cheerleader and imitating her hand motions. If she saw him, it didn't show.

Gabe passed through the open door, and cool air wrapped around him in a wave. No one spoke to him. At least no one's tripped me, yet. He slid off to a side, leaned against the wall, and watched students and teachers hurry by. He heard the rapid pounding of his heart in his ears and his knees barely supported him. He couldn't face that again. He concentrated on breathing deeply and slowly until he couldn't hear his heart anymore. He could do this. Short steps and keep his feet under him.

"You're Gabe Turner, aren't you?"

Gabe focused his eyes on the upper classman standing in front of him, Bobby Johnson who was student council president.

"Yes."

"Mr. Higgins told me you finished your Eagle project. My court of honor was just before homecoming last year."

"Way cool. What troop are you with?" Gabe stood up straight and started walking along with Bobby.

"Troop seventy-nine over in Green Oaks."

"I'm in Troop one ninety-eight at St. Andrew's."

"Yeah, I know you guys. You ran the zip line at the last jamboree."

A smile stretched Gabe's lips. "Yup, that's us."

"So when's your court of honor?"

"In a couple of weeks; you're welcome to come." Gabe stopped at his locker.

Bobby moved a couple of steps down the hall. "Let me know the date, maybe I will."

Gabe nodded. Bobby disappeared into the crowd and Gabe opened his locker. Maybe he would make it through this year okay.

*****

He walked out of geometry and pulled his schedule out of his pocket. 'A' lunch, and then he had to make the bus for Tech campus. He moved to the side of the crowd and headed for the cafeteria. The aromas wafted to his nose but a chill shook him. Daniel was not there. It would be different.

He inhaled a deep breath and held it until his head was ready to explode. He let it out slowly and pushed open the big swinging doors. He stepped into line and shuffled his way forward. It was a new lunch lady. She had blonde hair and wore a white hair net.

"What'll you have?" she asked.

"Two slices of cheese pizza."

"Would you like some salad? It comes with the pizza." She smiled and nodded encouragingly.

Salad was chick food, but it seemed important to her. It wouldn't kill him.

"Just a little, please." He lifted the plate of pizza to his tray and took the bowl of lettuce and tomato wedges from her. She gave him one more smile and turned to the next student in line.

He moved out into the seating area and looked for an empty spot. Bobby waved and motioned to an open seat at his table. Gabe hurried over and sat down.

"Gabe, this is Charlie, Charlene, Hannah and Joe. Everybody, this is Gabe." Bobby pointed to each person as he said each name. Everyone was a junior or a senior and all were on the student council.

Joe and Charlene waved, their mouths full of food. Charlie and Hannah offered hellos before taking their next bites of food.

Charlene picked up the conversation they'd been having before he joined them. "I agree homecoming needs some special decorations and a theme but I really think we need to rein things in a little." She took a bite of her taco.

"I don't know. My sister keeps teasing me we'll never top what they did last year for the winter formal. And she said the girls all love shopping for formals and getting dressed up." Joe said.

Hannah set down her hot dog. "Oh, yeah, just great. You go buy an expensive dress and get your boyfriend to match his tux and then you break up and sit home with a quart of Rocky Road ice cream."

Gabe laughed along with everyone else.

Bobby turned to him, "Gabe, we need an opinion not on the council. What do you think?"

Everyone turned to look at him. He swallowed his pizza with an audible gulp and sipped his lemonade. "I only went to one dance, the winter formal and I ended up shoveling snow for the rest of the winter to pay for it. I'm probably not the person to ask."

Charlene smiled at him and turned to Bobby. "Exactly. Isn't it time we stopped trying to one up the previous council and start thinking about the students we represent?"

"Point taken," Bobby said.

The bell rang and they all scrambled to stand up. Gabe followed Hannah up to dump his tray with Charlene right behind him.

"Thanks, for speaking up back there." Charlene said.

Gabe looked over his shoulder at her. "Glad to help. It's nice to know someone on the council is thinking about things like cost."

"It was the major plank of my campaign platform."

Gabe dropped his tray on the belt and stepped out of Charlene's way. "Are you planning on being a politician?"

She nodded her head up and down. "After I get my law degree, I'd like to run for the Senate some day. Bobby wants to run for Congress. What do you want to do?"

Here comes the point where she figures out I'm not in their league. "I'm planning on being an electrician."

She set her tray down and turned toward him. "Awesome. Hey would you want to run for student council? Bobby's and my seats come open after we graduate."

She meant it. "I don't think I'm popular enough."

"Think about it." Charlene turned then and slipped her arm through Bobby's as they headed for the far exit.

Gabe hurried out the closest door and scrambled onto the bus just before it pulled out. He dropped into a seat by himself and looked out the window. Was this a dream? Were they going to pull a trick on me like Jazz and Daniel?

This just couldn't be real.

CHAPTER 27

"Scouts. Scouts." The microphone made Mrs. Whitmore's voice flat. She stood at the podium; arms crossed and tapped her toe.

"Signs up." Gabe yelled. Groans answered him but everyone quieted and raised their hand.

"Charlie, you're first and light the scout candle." Mrs. Whitmore said.

"But I'm a second class scout."

"It can be your rank or a lower one for lighting the candles and we don't have any scouts in the troop with a rank under second class."

Charlie plunked down in a pew, crossed his arms over his chest and swung his feet. He wouldn't look up. Shane sat down next to him.

"Hey Charlie, don't worry, everyone who comes recognizes the rank insignias on your shirt. They'll all think you're cool for helping out and covering for scouts younger than you."

Charlie looked up at him. "Really?"

"Really." Shane smiled and walked away.

"What's my part again, Mrs. Whitmore?" Charlie skipped up to the podium.

She smiled and turned the page of the script. "Right here. When I say,' the Scout begins his journey' you stand up and light the Scout candle."

Gabe grabbed Shane's sleeve and pulled him toward the back of the sanctuary. "Excuse me but when have you been to an Eagle Court of Honor?"

"This will be my first, but Charlie doesn't need to know that. All he needs to know is that people won't think less of him or wonder why he hasn't advanced in rank when he has." Shane smiled. "I'm up." He walked to the front of the sanctuary and lit the candle for First Class.

*****

Gabe stood in the parking lot. The sun warmed his face. It was getting cooler. The leaves were starting to turn color. White lacy clouds streaked the blue bowl of sky. His dad motioned him to the truck. He hopped in and buckled his seat belt. They pulled out of the driveway but turned the wrong way.

"Where are we going?"

"We're meeting your mother at the O'Hara's place."

"Why?"

"You'll see." His dad turned the radio way up making further conversation impossible. His dad never listened to the radio unless he needed to hear the weather.

Now what?

Five minutes later his dad signaled and turned into the O'Hara's steep driveway. The truck climbed it with a roar. Gabe climbed out and waited for his father to come around the truck. An old black mini-pick up, spotted with rust sat in the driveway.

"That's not the O'Hara's' truck. I wonder who's here."

"Come here." His dad motioned him over to the other vehicle a grin coming and going across his face.

Gabe walked over, glancing from side to side. Where is everybody?

"Surprise!" His mom and the O'Haras darted out from behind the garage.

"I know it's a beater, son, but it's got a good engine and brakes. You'll have to find a way to help with the insurance before you can drive it, but as soon as you turn sixteen, this is your truck." His dad dropped the ignition key into Gabe's hand.

Gabe stared at the key and then at the truck. "It's mine?" He looked from the key to the truck and back to his father. "I have my own truck?"

His dad grinned and nodded. Gabe reached for the door handle, yanked it open and climbed into the driver's seat. He hung onto the steering wheel and touched the various gages and controls.

Shane climbed into the passenger seat. "Start it up."

Gabe glanced at his father and turned the key. The engine roared to life.

"Yes!" Gabe laughed and Shane joined in.

His dad closed the door and rested his hands on the open window frame. "Buckle up and take it around the pasture here a few times."

"It's okay?"

"Just don't try taking it out on the road." His dad stepped back and put his arm around Mom's shoulders.

Gabe stepped on the clutch and shifted into first gear. Slowly he let the clutch out. The engine sputtered and almost died. He pressed harder on the gas pedal and the truck jerked forward about six feet.

"Whoa."

He eased up pressure with his right foot and steered between a couple of trees and out into the big mowed field. By the third lap he had the feel for the engine and shifted smoothly up and down. His face ached from smiling. He pulled up by the garage and parked the truck. He jumped out and hugged his dad and then his mom.

"Thank you. I can't believe you did this. I always figured I'd need to save up for my first car."

"We found a great deal and we wanted to give you something really special for an Eagle present," his mom said.

"Thank you." Gabe looked over his mom's shoulder. Shane watched him and gave a thumb up sign.

"Well, God, I never thought things would work out this way. I'll leave getting them to church up to You. Let me know if I can help."

CHAPTER 28

Gabe glanced around the clearing. The bright yellow of the leaves collected and intensified what little sunlight came from the overcast sky. The rich smells of damp earth and fallen leaves riding the cool breeze made him suck it in big gulps and savor it like a piece of hard candy.

He waited for Babe, the red cong on the yellow rope readily available in his lap. He glanced at his watch. After one, Brian's been searching for me for two hours. He was getting hungry.

He shifted position and leaned back using his pack as a pillow. He tipped his hat over his eyes and dozed. A small rustling, a strong draft and then a big paw landed square on his thigh. Babe had the cong in his mouth ready to take off.

"Oh no you don't," Gabe closed his hand on the rope just before Babe pulled it out of range. The dog jerked him from flat on his back over onto his stomach. "You've got to alert to get your play. Drop it."

Babe spit out the cong and pounded the ground in excitement. Gabe smiled and made eye contact but said nothing as he climbed to his feet. Babe started to bark in a steady rhythm.

"Okay, reward him." Brian's voice came over the radio.

Gabe moved the cong a fraction of an inch and Babe had it in his teeth again. Gabe tugged. Babe yanked him forward a step. He dug in his heels and pulled the dog toward him only to have Babe give him another jerk.

"Base from unit three, subject found in good condition. Returning to base, ETA fifteen minutes."

Gabe glanced up to see Brian talking into the radio mike. Babe took advantage of his distraction and yanked the cong out of his hands.

"Good boy, Babe." The dog trotted over to his handler and leaned while Brian petted and stroked the big creature.

Gabe collected his pack and glanced around for any trash he might have dropped. "Babe would make a great clock, instead of tick tock it would be woof woof."

"Right, and how would anyone hear themselves think?"

"Good point." Gabe tightened his pack waist belt and nodded. "How much lunch do you think they left for us?"

"Probably not enough. I'm starved." Brian smiled and motioned Babe to range.

Gabe grinned and grabbed his pack straps to hold them steady. "Race ya.'" He took off down the trail with Brian's footsteps pounding behind him and Babe running big circles around them both.

"Hey, Gabe, can you give me a hand?" Mrs. O'Hara had Clara on a leash and walked toward a fifteen foot long two by twelve spanning two saw horses.

"Sure," Gabe swerved away from the base tent and walked toward her. Brian saluted him and disappeared through the white flap. "What do you need me to do?"

"I need to teach Clara to turn around on the plank. I need you on the far side to catch her if she falls off."

Gabe stepped in close to the board and watched as Clara negotiated the ladder up to the wooden surface. "Why does she need this?"

"On a disaster site you need to be able to direct the dog away from danger it can't see but you can, so you teach the command Turn."

Gabe watched Mrs. O'Hara.

"Good girl. Stay. Forward. Stay. Forward. Turn." Gabe moved

swiftly as the dog teetered and wobbled and barely managed to change directions on the narrow board.

"Good girl. Forward." The red sable shepherd scurried down the ladder to the ground. Mrs. O'Hara pulled a tug from her pocket. Clara lunged, clamping her strong jaw around the toy and tugging hard.

Mrs. O'Hara laughed and tugged back. "Thanks, Gabe. Go ahead and have lunch."

He headed for the food tent, the play sounds behind him gradually diminished. So was that what God did for him? Taught him how to turn away from danger. He would try and remember it.

*****

Gabe climbed into the front seat of the truck and adjusted the vent toward his face. The truck felt like a sauna after the whole day in the woods. He folded his arms across his chest and watched the sun set in a flood of orange, magenta, and purple.

"Looks like the team's going to be ready for the evaluation, no problems." His dad shifted the truck into gear and followed the big white base camp down the haul road.

"When's it going to happen?"

"Next month." His dad slowed the truck and waited while Mr. O'Hara pulled out onto the main road. "Mom and I talked about what you asked us to do for an Eagle present."

"It's okay, Dad. I didn't understand. I didn't mean to make you remember. I just wanted you to find what I had." Gabe glanced at his father's face. The setting sun changed his Dad's coloring and he looked more like a stone sculpture than a person.

Silence filled the truck. His dad changed lanes and signaled for a left turn. Once around the corner the trees blocked the last of the sunset and the interior of the truck filled with shadows.

"What did you find?" his dad asked quietly.

"Peace. A safe place. A feeling I belonged somewhere and more than family cared about me." Gabe stared straight ahead. He couldn't make himself turn toward his dad and see the hurt.

"Your mom was right."

His head snapped around. "About what?"

"You're more comfortable in your own skin than ever before."

Gabe let out a sigh. "I love you and Mom too much to ever deliberately hurt you. I can't imagine how bad it must make you feel every time I leave to go to services, so I'm not going to go anymore. We can let the subject drop. I won't bring it up again."

His dad glanced away from the road and looked at him. "I'll survive." He turned back to the road. "If you want to stop going because you have other things you want to do more, then stop going. But if you want to go and don't to protect your mom and me, then I'll drag you there and shove you in the door, myself."

Gabe swallowed the lump in his throat. He couldn't speak.

"Your mom thinks we've waited long enough. Maybe this church is different then the other one. She's planning on going with you when she gets a Sunday off."

His hands and feet tingled. Butterflies filled his stomach. "The Sunday school kids sang a song for the congregation. It said the church wasn't a building, it was the people gathered there. I think you'll like these people. I couldn't see them treating anyone the way the other minister did you."

His dad sighed. "You're probably right, but I need a little more time. I just can't walk in there yet. I don't fully understand how your mom can manage it. You will understand if it gets too much for her?"

"If I see any sign that she's upset, I'll take her out of there."

"Good, then I don't have to worry about her." His dad lapsed into silence.

"So God, in Your own good time this will happen. Thanks. Amen," Gabe whispered.

CHAPTER 29

"Hey, Gabe." Hannah waved both hands back and forth over her head.

He nodded and headed her way, carrying his lunch bag in one hand and a bunch of papers in the other. "Here are the drawings you asked for."

"I can't tell you how much this helps. We don't have anyone on the council who can do CAD drawings." She spread them out in the center of the table. Gabe pulled his sandwich back out of the way to give her more room.

Bobby and Charlene slipped their trays partway onto the table and look at the drawings spread out in front of them.

Bobby sat down. "Now I see what you were getting at. This'll be really cool looking."

"The best part is it won't cost hardly anything." Charlene added.

Joe joined the group. "The real money saver was Gabe's idea to have a disc jockey contest for all the dances this year. The equipment rental is a tenth of the cost to hire someone, and people get to practice their skills on a live audience." He sat down and faced Gabe. "So who are you bringing to homecoming?"

Gabe choked on his sandwich, visions of Jazz and Daniel laughing played in his mind. He wasn't risking that again. "No one. I'm saving up my money so I can buy car insurance."

"That's such a guy thing. They'd rather work on greasy old cars than go to a dance." Hannah said.

Charlene nodded and laughed. Bobby, Joe and Gabe exchanged glances. Bobby shrugged and sat down. Gabe bit off a piece of tuna. If I keep my mouth full they can't ask me any more tough questions.

"If we work on it for the next two weeks we should have plenty of paper snowflakes cut out. I wish we could get some flowers." Hannah said.

"Remember, we want the cost at $15 per student attending. If we buy flowers we'll go over what we expect to bring in." Joe warned.

Hannah pretended to pout and batted her eyelashes at him. "Isn't there some way we could manage it?"

Gabe swallowed a gulp of soda. "If you don't think it's ghoulish, there is."

All four people spun toward him.

"What?" Bobby asked.

Go to funeral homes and hospitals and ask for the flower arrangements they're throwing out. Pull them out of the arrangements and make up your own."

"You're right," Bobby said. "Our troop did that to decorate for our medieval faire. Only the people doing the pick up knew, and the place looked great."

"Now that's what I call being thrifty." Charlene joked. "I'll start calling after school tonight."

Bobby swallowed. "I'd still like to link this in with a canned goods drive for the local shelter. The question is, how much can we afford to knock off the door price?"

"It would make sense, the lower we can get the price, the more people will attend. We have to pay for the security staff and the equipment rental. The cheerleaders are going to run a concessions stand for food so we don't have to worry about buying soda and stuff." Joe said.

"That from the guy who came in second at the hot dog eating contest." Hannah winked.

Joe scrunched up his face and grabbed his stomach. "Don't remind me. The thought of a hot dog is more than I can take."

Gabe laughed along with everyone else.

"We don't have the up front cost of buying food but we also don't make any profit from it either." Charlene said.

The bell rang and Gabe scrambled to his feet, folding the lunch bag at the same time.

"Remember, we all meet here after school two weeks from tonight to decorate." Bobby turned to Gabe. "We could use someone with your reach if you can make it."

"That'd be fun. I'd like to, as long as it's not snowing I can do it. Otherwise I need to take care of my customers first." Gabe headed for the exit. He needed to grab his coat before getting on the bus to Tech.

CHAPTER 30

"Gabe, get the big frying pan from the truck," Dad said.

Gabe nodded and climbed into the base camp. He grabbed the action packer labeled "cookware" and rummaged inside until he came up with the heavy cast iron skillet. He glanced out the front window of the truck to see a car pulling into the parking lot.

Grabbing hold of the doorframe he leaned as far around as he could. "Here, Dad. We have some civilians who just pulled in."

His dad made a circle of olive oil on the surface and scraped the onions he'd chopped into the pan. He set it on an unlit burner and wiped his hands on a towel. "Mrs. O'Hara said the daughter of a coworker wanted to come out and help. Said she'll probably be totally out of her element, so we need to keep an eye on her and make sure the cold doesn't get to her. I better go say hello."

His dad walked out of the tent. Gabe watched through the opening. A couple and a girl had gotten out of the car and Mrs. O'Hara talked to them. The couple walked away, although the man turned back once to say something. The girl stood there, her arms wrapped around herself and even took a step toward where the car had been.

"She's scared. Been there, done that," Gabe said.

He reached for the flap, to walk over to her. Mrs. O'Hara motioned the girl over to the O'Hara SUV and started tossing clothes at her. He dropped the flap back and went to light the burner under the onions. He unwrapped the ground turkey and added it to the pan as his father returned. Within half an hour they had the chili simmering on the stove and big hunks of Italian bread cut up and ready for dipping.

Shane came in and poured himself a cup of hot chocolate. "Mom and the new girl are back and Dad's collecting everyone outside."

Gabe dusted the crumbs off his hands and reached for his coat. "I'd better go to the briefing." He grabbed two Styrofoam cups and filled each with hot liquid. He hurried outside and joined the group collecting around Mr. O'Hara. She stood in front of Brian.

"Everyone, this is Blanca Martinez. She's volunteered to help out and play subject. Be nice so she'll come back." Mr. O'Hara said.

"Hi Blanca, glad to have you, but didn't your mother teach you to come in out of the cold?"

She spun around her eyes flashing. She's ready to take a chunk out of Brian; good for her. Maybe she'll be a keeper.

Brian laughed. Sticking out a gloved hand he said, "Hi, I'm Brian, welcome to the team." She shook his hand and laughed. She turned back as Mr. O'Hara started to explain the practice scenario.

Gabe squeezed between Bianca and Brian and reaching over her shoulder handed her a cup of hot chocolate. She spun around and faced his chest. She looked up, "Thanks".

She's got the most beautiful eyes I've ever seen. They're the color of a chocolate bar with flecks of gold. He swallowed and clamped his jaw shut and looked up at Mr. O'Hara hoping that he wouldn't do anything lastingly stupid.

"Shane, you're out for Babe first. Gabe you'll take Blanca and go for Taz." Mr. O'Hara said. "Any questions?" He glanced around at people. "Let's get to work, we're burning daylight."

Blanca glanced around and hesitated. She chewed on the end of her mitten.

Did Gabe ever know what she was feeling!

"Blanca, come with me." Gabe hurried over to his Dad's truck, opened the back hatch and rummaged for blankets and tarps.

"Do you live in that thing?" she asked.

Laughter bubbled out of his chest. "Sort of, Shane and I are boy scouts and our dads are assistant troop leaders. We do a lot of camping so there's always extra stuff in the trucks in case someone in the troop needs something. Did you bring anything warm to wrap up in while we're waiting to be found?"

She shook her head no.

He grabbed a tarp and blanket and stuffed them into an old back pack. "Put this on." She slipped her arms through and he coughed to hide his laugh. He adjusted straps so the pack fit her much smaller frame. He saw Shane coming and winked at her. "Shane likes to take a sleeping bag, but that's because he's too skinny to stay warm in a blanket."

"Who you calling skinny, fat boy?" Shane pretended to elbow him in the stomach. Gabe wrapped him up in a wrestling hold that he knew Shane could get out of.

"Finally, someone who doesn't tower over me," she said.

Gabe fell down and rolled on the ground with laughter as Shane pretended to scowl.

"I'm sorry." Tears welled up in her eyes.

Shane stopped scowling. "Hey, no problem, it's just these overgrown lumps can get pretty annoying sometimes when they tower over you. Us normal people will have to stick together and take 'em down a notch or two. Wait until we get into dense brush, then you'll see the advantage to being small."

"Don't worry Shane, you'll grow and then you'll have to duck brambles and branches, too."

"Shane?" Mrs. O'Hara called.

Shane hurried over to her.

"How old is he?" Blanca turned to Gabe.

"Twelve- and a really good friend."

"Subjects, come get radios." Mr. O'Hara yelled.

Gabe motioned Blanca to follow him. He took the radio Mr. O'Hara handed him and passed it to Blanca. "Make sure this dial is on one and turn this knob to adjust the volume." He pointed with a gloved finger. "Press this one to talk and let go to listen. Make sure your pack doesn't press on it or you cut off communications for the whole team."

"Got a radio check for me, Gabe?" Mr. O'Hara asked with a smile.

"Base from subject Gabe, radio check." Gabe heard his voice coming over the base radio and turned and nodded to Blanca.

"Subject Blanca from base, radio check." She spoke too softly for the radio to pick up and her voice shook slightly.

Gabe smiled. "Pretty close. You have to talk loud for the radios to pick it up clearly and always say who you want to talk to first, then identify yourself."

"Base from subject Blanca, radio check."

He heard her voice coming from the base radio. "Good."

"Let's go." Mr. O'Hara headed out the trail. "Shane go three hundred yards on a heading of five degrees."

Shane nodded and disappeared into the trees. They followed the trail for a few more minutes. "Gabe, go a hundred and fifty yards on a heading of one seventy-five. You're the Eagle Scout, Blanca is the novice. I trust you to take good care of her."

Gabe's face filled with heat. He nodded, pulled out his compass got his heading and took off, counting paces under his breath. He stopped and glanced around. They were on the edge of a small clearing, about ten feet in diameter. "We're here."

"Now what?" she asked.

He could barely hear her soft voice.

"We wait for Taz to find us. It might be a while." Gabe glanced around the clearing. "This log looks pretty good. Use your hands and stir up the leaves into a big pile and spread your tarp over them." He used his long arms to help her collect them. "Now wrap up in your blanket and sit on the tarp."

She followed his directions and sank down in the center of the leaves, her back against the downed trunk. He reached out and wrapped the tarp up over her head and around her.

"Good, you look like a blue mummy."

She laughed. "What about you?"

Gabe quickly created his own leaf bed and sat down.

She laughed again. "I see what you mean about the mummy."

Silence. "Where do you go to school?" he asked.

"I'm a freshman at Carmel. You?"

"Sophomore at Indian Hill."

"Did you learn all this stuff from scouting?"

"Some of it. Some of it we learned from the search team. They really like to help. If you get stuck on some school work ask them, their really big on doing good in school." Gabe reached out between the edges of his tarp to pick up a stick.

"I'm okay on the math but the English lit makes me crazy." She rolled her eyes.

"Tell me about it. Mr. O'Hara helped me big time there." He drew designs in the dirt. Silence filled the clearing once more.

"Do you miss going to church when you go to search practice?" she asked.

"A little. I've only just started going to services. The O'Haras take me with them," he answered.

"Your parents don't make you go?" Her eyes had gotten really big.

"They had a bad experience and haven't gone for a really long time."

"What happened?"

"I had a baby sister who died and the minister said it was because they didn't have enough faith."

She half stood up. Her face paled and she shook so the tarp vibrated. "How could he do something so mean? Your parents needed love and help."

"I don't understand it, either. Mom has decided she's going to start coming to church with me but my dad isn't ready. I don't know what to say to make it better for him." Gabe looked at the ground. Why did he open up to her? Would she use it to hurt him?

"My friend Carla's baby sister got killed in a drive by shooting. At the funeral the priest talked about how Lazarus had died and Jesus wept with his sister Mary. He raised Lazarus

from the dead to show us we'd all be raised in the resurrection."
She stopped and wiped at the tears on her face. "He said Jesus
wept with us too at the death of this child and offered us the
comfort of being reunited with her in the resurrection. Maybe
you could share that story with him and it'd help."

Gabe's stomach hit his feet. It's the answer Dad needed.
"Do you know where it is in the Bible?"

"Someplace in the book of John."

"Are you upset at not going to church?" he asked.

"No. It's another place I don't feel like I belong. Moving
out of the city was supposed to fix everything. Instead everything
is so much worse." She quietly dug in the leaves with her own
stick. "I used to love going to our old church. The minister's
deep voice was what I imagined God would sound like if he
spoke out loud to us. Here it's different and feels strange."

"Don't you think God is listening to you any more?"

"I know that He's listening. He's always been there. I don't
know how I know, I just know, He's always there for me, no
matter what. He and Mama are the only constants I can always
count on."

"What about your Dad?"

"I love Papa and he loves me, but I can't talk to him and I
can't do anything right as far as he's concerned. He wants me to
quit school and get married, but I'm not ready to be a mother yet."

Pain filled Gabe's chest. Great, I start to get interested in
another girl and she already has a boyfriend. "What does your
boyfriend want to do?"

"I don't have one. I don't understand me and my dreams,
so how can I know who I should spend the rest of my life with?
I want to go to college. Mama wants me to be an engineer but
working with machines doesn't interest me. I don't know what
I want. So how can I know who to marry?"

The ice in his chest melted. "My dad wanted me to go to
college but I've decided to be an electrician."

"How did you figure it out?"

"Scouting."

"Do you think the boy scouts will let me in? I could cut my hair really short." She squinted her eyes as she laughed.

"Your hair is too beautiful to cut short."

Gabe was surprised that he said that out loud.

Taz appeared through the bushes, turned around and left. Gabe put his finger to his lips as he saw Blanca open her mouth to speak. A few seconds later Mrs. O'Hara stood in the clearing. Gabe gathered up the treats and petted and rough housed with Taz and fed her liver.

"Let's head back to base," Mrs. O'Hara said. "Lunch should be about ready."

Gabe gathered his tarp and blanket and trotted off with Taz.

"I hope she forgets what I said about her hair," he said to himself, all the while wishing that she would definitely remember.

CHAPTER 31

Gabe walked through the mall with Bobby and Joe. Bobby carried a list of items they needed to pick up as gag gifts for the donkey basketball game next week.

"Oh man, look. Southface is going out of business."

Bobby and Joe turned in the direction Gabe pointed.

"I'm not surprised." Joe said, "I don't know anyone around here who uses camping and climbing stuff."

"Speak for yourself." Bobby pretended to threaten Joe with a fist. "You're with two boy scouts, remember? I love looking around in there."

"Come on, let's go in." Gabe took a step toward the entrance.

"Charlene will kill us if we don't get all the stuff on this list tonight." Bobby tilted his head and used a warning tone.

"Hey, she's your girlfriend, not ours." Joe laughed. "Let's go, Gabe."

Gabe walked around the store. Compasses were twenty-five percent off. Coats were eighty percent off. Did Blanca know about this?

"Hey this is great." Bobby waved him over. "We can get stuff like freeze dried ice cream as some of the gifts on this list."

"It's not bad if you can find really cold water to mix it up." Gabe reached out and sorted through flavors.

"Yuck. Of course the only time I had some, it was imitation

banana flavor. I'll take a good old dump cake, any day."

"I'm with you, there." Gabe said.

"What's a dump cake?" Joe asked, "Doesn't sound too appetizing."

Bobby flung an arm around Joe's shoulders, "You have no idea. It's called a dump cake because you just dump everything into a pan and bake it."

Gabe's mouth watered. "I'll try and save you a piece after next search practice."

Joe crossed his eyes, "Don't do me any favors."

"Let's check out." Bobby said.

*****

Gabe pulled the folded up slip of paper out of his wallet and smoothed it open on his desk. His hands shook slightly as he dialed the number.

"Bueno."

I hope she speaks English. "Uh, Mrs. Martinez? This is Gabe Turner from the search group. May I speak to Blanca?"

"Hi Gabe, hang on just a minute. "Muffled noise and voices came through the telephone.

"Hello?"

"Hey, Blanca, it's Gabe. Are you coming back to training next Sunday?"

"Yeah. I can't wait. I'm practicing with my compass all the time."

"Be careful around iron or magnets, they draw the needle off North." Gabe drew a circle on his desk with the tip of his finger.

"They do? So that explains why it's working funny in school."

"You took your compass to school?"

"Hey, I need all the practice I can get if I'm going to at least be as good as Shane."

"If you're as good as Shane, you'll be an expert."

"Why? Is Shane some compass wiz kid?"

"Sort of, he's been doing this two years longer than I have and he's really close to getting his Eagle rank in scouting."

"Wait a minute, isn't that your rank?"

"Yup. Only four out of a hundred scouts make it and he'll have it by the time he's thirteen."

"Okay, I'm impressed. So how long has he been doing this scouting thing?"

"Well, he moved up from cub scouts when he was eleven. The thing of it is he's been out with the search group so long he does a lot of advanced scout stuff and doesn't know it's supposed to be hard."

"So how old was he when he started with the search training?"

"Eight."

"You're kidding!"

"Nope, he has a leg up on us."

"So what's up?"

"There's a big sale going on over at the climbing shop in the mall."

"Yeah, I saw it was going out of business."

"Go check it out, compasses and really good gear are going to be the cheapest you'll ever see them. If you're not sure about something, give my dad or me a call."

"Thanks."

Gabe hit the disconnect button on the telephone.

Yes! She was coming back.

CHAPTER 32

"Come on Gabe, you haven't been to a single dance all year." Hannah stood next to him in the hallway, her lips pressed together and hands on her hips.

"What's it to you?" Gabe tried to back away but bumped up against the wall.

"You're a nice guy. You could be really popular if you let yourself relax a little more." She took a small step forward and raised her hands as if in supplication.

"I want you to run for student council. You have some really good ideas and you made a difference this year. If you don't run, Joe and I'll get stuck with some of those plastic Barbie's. All they're interested in is they're own little clique not the school in general." She pointed to Jazz and her friends as they walked by.

"How does going to the dance make a difference?"

"You go to class and Tech and that's it. Nobody knows you so no one will vote for you. If you go to the dance, people can talk to you and figure out Gabe the person not Gabe the A student hiding in the back of the room."

"Did you ever think I don't want to be on the student council?"

"Why? I thought you had fun with us?" Her mouth turned down and her eyes reminded him of Taz when she got scolded.

He exhaled a deep breath. "I do have fun but I just don't

think I'll get very many votes and I'm not up for that kind of punishment."

He closed his eyes to get them to stop watering. "I can see the signs now, 'Vote for the janitor's kid,-he knows where the mops are stored."

Hannah reached out and rested her hand on his shoulder.

"The signs would read, 'Vote for the Eagle Scout who makes school events fun and affordable'.

"People are voting for you and what you can do for them. Your dad isn't the one to sit on the council."

"Thanks, Hannah." Gabe turned to go into his next class.

Hannah grabbed his wrist. "Even if you don't run, please come to the dance. We miss you."

Gabe walked into history and slid into his seat. He didn't want to go to the dance alone. Would Blanca be willing to go? He would ask her at search practice.

*****

Gabe reached into the crate. The puppy ducked under his hands in a bid for freedom. He barely caught its hips before the black and tan fur-ball escaped. He couldn't let go or she would be free and he couldn't reach the collar.

Her laugh reached him first, and then she had a leash on the collar and she lifted the squirming bundle into her arms. The bill of her hat cast a shadow across her face, her hood pulled up over it for added protection from the rain.

One look at her smile and Gabe forgot the drops running down his face and chilling his skin. Wow, she was beautiful.

"Go grab the other one, I've got this little girl." She laughed again. "When these two are done we can get some hot chocolate."

Gabe walked toward the other crate but stopped as a tan van slowly pulled into the parking lot. Shane came over intent on finishing puppy training. Gabe looked up, punched Shane in the shoulder to get his attention, pointed and laughed.

"I don't know who they are, but they're going to be hypothermic in about five minutes out here. Incoming – potential ice cubes." Shane looked around and laughed too.

"Shut up Gabe, I want to see that girl try and walk the trails in those high heels. Betcha a Coke that she gets stuck before she makes the tree line."

"Take her." Blanca shoved the puppy she'd been holding into his arms and hurried toward the new comers.

Gabe exchanged glances with Shane. "What do you think is going on?"

"I don't know but my little voice says Blanca needs help." The hard line of Shane's jaw spoke volumes.

Gabe shoved the puppy back into the crate leash and all. Mr. O'Hara and his dad converged on the newcomers. Mrs. O'Hara was already there. Gabe watched her gently push Blanca behind her and cross her arms over her chest. Oh, really not good. He hurried over to the group along with Brian. They came up quietly behind the women. Gabe positioned himself so he could push Blanca out of the way if fists started flying.

Mrs. O'Hara put her arm around Blanca's shoulders and maneuvered her toward the base camp and away from the newcomers. Gabe stepped between her and the strangers as Mr. O'Hara put the guy in a wrist lock and steered him toward the van. His dad stepped really close to the girl, towering over her. Brian moved in beside Dad and they used their combined size to force her to back-track without touching her. Gabe hurried around them and opened the passenger door for the girl. He heard Mr. O'Hara speaking softly to the driver while still holding the stranger's wrist.

"I used to break other peoples' bones for a living. I was good at it and got paid real well. More than one person has offered me a lot of money to come out of retirement. I haven't taken them up on it, but you show up here again and I'll make an exception for the pleasure of busting you up. You come near anyone on this team again, I'll do more than break bones, and with our training we can hide the bodies so no one will ever find them. Comprendez?"

The guy's face was white and he swallowed hard. Gabe glanced at Mr. O'Hara's hand. It moved slightly and the stranger moaned.

"Do you understand me?" Gabe saw Mr. O'Hara's eyes change color, just like Shane's had done during the fight. Gabe swallowed hard. This looked like one of the moves Shane hadn't shared with him.

The stranger nodded his head. "Yes."

"Good boy. Maybe you aren't as dumb as you look." Mr. O'Hara released him and slammed the driver door. Gabe followed suit and stepped back away from the vehicle. They drove off in a cloud of blue smoke.

The men watched until the van disappeared from sight. A movement caught Gabe's attention and he saw Shane disappearing into the base camp with a puppy in his arms. "What just happened?"

Mr. O'Hara let out a sigh. "Blanca got into the wrong crowd at school for a while. She realized her mistake and made a clean break from them before there were any serious problems. Her parents warned us they were the kind to make trouble, so we've half been expecting this."

His dad nodded. "It'd been so long we had pretty much figured they were going to leave her alone. That poor girl has got to feel awful."

"I'd like to go cheer her up." Gabe said.

Shane stepped out of the base camp. His dad motioned him over. "How is she?"

"Crying like there's no tomorrow. She told Mom to call her parents before she ruins this for everyone." Shane's mouth turned down and he furrowed his brow.

"Everybody, leave her alone and go back to work. Shane, Gabe head for the field." Mr. O'Hara ordered.

*****

Gabe took off his coat and threw it into the back of his Dad's truck and peeled off his soggy sweat shirt. He twisted it between his hands wringing water out of the dark folds as he watched Blanca get into her parent's car and drive away. He grabbed a dry fleece out of the back and walked over to help take down the tent. "Is she doing any better?"

"A little. She's blaming herself for things outside her control." Mrs. O'Hara shook her head. "My guess is she's going to walk away from the team to try and protect us."

Gabe's stomach hit his feet. "We can't let her."

"How do we stop it?"

Gabe smile. "Time for rank advancement."

"What do you mean?"

"She loves dogs and would give anything, do almost anything to be a handler someday. Isn't there some way you can make that happen?"

Mrs. O'Hara looked at the ground and rubbed her chin with a knuckle. A puppy yipped and she glanced over at the crates and slowly smiled.

"Handler no, junior handler, yes." She looked up at him. "You've got something there and I've got work to do."

They walked over to the tent. Gabe grabbed one side of the wet nylon and started folding.

Mrs. O'Hara loaded the big plastic bins called action packers while Shane carried them to the shelves. "How do you guys feel about doing some PR at Blanca's school?"

"What do you have in mind?" Mr. O'Hara asked as he folded a table.

"The school news letter said there would be an assembly to honor students for their service work. How would you feel about announcing Blanca as a junior handler there?"

"Do you think they'd do it? We're not affiliated with the school in any way." Brian unlatched the table legs and folded them in.

"I like the idea, do you think we can get her a uniform and present it to her there?" Gabe's dad grabbed the other end of the table and helped carry it to the truck.

"Can we give her one of the puppies?" Shane asked. "Collette's already bonded to her and vice versa."

"That may be a tough one. I have to talk to her mother." Mrs. O'Hara said. "What do your school schedules look like? Do you two think you could get out for an afternoon to act as escort?"

Shane grinned, "An afternoon off? I'm in."

Mrs. O'Hara rolled her eyes and shook her head, then turned to Gabe.

"I'm in. All I have is a dance that night." Gabe said. A thump off to the side made him glance around. His dad had dropped his end of the second table.

"Are you taking Blanca?" Shane asked.

Heat crept up Gabe's neck and face. Shane was his friend but right now Gabe wanted to strangle him. "I was thinking about it, but I never got the chance to ask."

Shane winked and made a wide circle around him into the truck with the next action packer. He knew that he better stay out of Gabe's reach.

"If you call to ask her, don't tell her what we have planned." Mrs. O'Hara warned. She slammed the back door of the base camp closed and headed for her SUV.

Gabe climbed into the passenger seat of his Dad's truck and savored the heat. His dad took his position behind the wheel. "I'm glad you've decided to go to the dance."

"My friends will be there. I just hope Blanca will go with me. I don't want to go alone."

"Are there any girls in your school you could take?"

"No. I trust Blanca. If she can't go, I'll skip the dance." He turned to look at his Dad. "If she can go, you'll need to drive us; it ends after curfew."

His dad broke into a big smile. "No problem at all."

*****

Shane tucked in his class A shirt and adjusted his boy scout sash. "Were you able to get hold of Blanca?"

Gabe adjusted his neckerchief and put on the slide. "No and I called every day for two weeks."

"Bummer. What are you going to do?"

"Ask her after the presentation." Gabe peeked out between the curtains and watched the students trickle into the auditorium. The bell rang and a crush of students filled the doorways. "Come on. We have to get into position or we'll never find her in this crowd."

Slowly they made their way up the left side of the auditorium. Gabe scanned the crowd. He caught sight of her just as the presentations started and motioned for Shane to follow him. Quietly they slipped up behind Blanca.

The superintendent stepped to the microphone. "We have always encouraged our students to give of their time and effort to help others in our community. We have several programs here at the school and we try to recognize the participants regularly. Occasionally, very special individuals go outside these programs. One such individual has come to our attention.

"When the president of the organization called me early this week and explained what was going on and asked if they could make a special presentation when we had finished honoring the other award recipients. I thought that it was a wonderful opportunity to remind our student body of the importance of volunteering in whatever manner you are able. It is with great pleasure I present the German Shepherd Search and Rescue Dog Association."

All the students erupted into applause and whistles as the dogs and handlers walked on stage. Gabe's father stepped to the microphone.

"Honor Guard, escort our new member and her parents forward."

"Surprise," Gabe said, "March victim."

"Subject, victims are the ones we don't look for." Blanca smiled over her shoulder at him.

"There aren't a large number of people we invite to our trainings. There are even fewer we invite to become a member of the team, so it is with great pleasure that I present to this fine young woman membership in German Shepherd Search and Rescue Dog Association."

Gabe's dad handed Blanca a certificate and shook her hand. "In addition to the certificate, we would also like to present Blanca with a unit uniform." He handed her the blue pants, shirt and fleece that the unit members wore on searches.

Mr. O'Hara stepped up to the microphone and Gabe's dad stepped back. "Blanca, we decided to go way out on a limb here. This is Colette and the unit has purchased her to train for Search and Rescue. We talked to your parents, and they have agreed to let you raise her for the first year and do the play drive training." Mr. O'Hara scooped up the puppy and stuffed her into Blanca's arms. It immediately slurped her face.

The students laughed. The superintendent returned to the microphone.

"Assembly dismissed." She stepped over to talk to Mrs. O'Hara.

Gabe reached out and caught Blanca's fleece. It had slipped from her grasp as she struggled to hold the puppy. "Hey, Blanca, do you think your parents would let you go to a school dance with me tonight?"

"Tonight, I don't know, it's kind of short notice." She glanced over at her father.

"Well, next time, take my calls and it won't be short notice."

Blanca blushed, and turned to her father. Just then Colette twisted in her arms and tried to play tug with one of Gabe's merit badges.

"Hey, wait a minute, puppy, that's not a toy." Gabe gently freed the badge and stepped back. He looked up to see Blanca's father nod yes and smile.

"Yes. I'm going to a dance with a babe," Gabe thought.

CHAPTER 33

Gabe walked up the path and rang the door bell. He turned and glanced back at his dad in the truck and reached up to straighten his collar. The door opened.

"Hi Mr. Martinez. Is Blanca ready?"

The man motioned him in the door with a smile, "let me call her."

Gabe glanced at a movement on the stairs. First he saw a flash of pale color and then a slender leg. Blanca came into view, looking so lovely in a pink party dress, her hair pinned up into an intricate braid. He stepped over to the stairs to take her hand as she came down the last two steps. "Wow. You look so beautiful. I've never seen you in anything but jeans and sweat shirts. "

Oh what a stupid thing to say!

"I mean you always look pretty; it's just you look really gorgeous now." That didn't come out right, either. Gabe felt heat climbing up his neck and face.

Blanca looked up at him and smiled. "Thank you. You look very handsome in your good clothes, too."

He glanced up to see her father frowning at him. He straightened and focused on him even though he wanted to stare at her.

"My dad's waiting in the truck. He's going to drive us to and from the dance. I won't let anything happen to her, sir."

Mr. Martinez looked over at Blanca and said something in rapid Spanish. She had been staring at Gabe. He'd felt her eyes watching him. She turned to her father and lost her smile.

"Si, Papa."

Sounds like he just told her off. What's going on? "Mr. Martinez?" The man turned to face him. "The dance ends at midnight and it takes about twenty minutes to get here. Blanca should be home by twelve thirty if that's all right with you."

"Si, twelve thirty will be fine but no later. I have to get up in the morning for work and I will be waiting up."

"Papa, you have to get up at five, you don't have to wait up."

Gabe smiled, "Yes, he does. He's your father and he's going to worry until you're home and back in his care."

Mr. Martinez smiled at him. "You understand."

Gabe nodded and opened the door for Blanca. "Good night, sir."

Blanca took his arm and strolled down the walk. At least I don't have to be embarrassed about my Dad's truck with her.

Gabe opened the door and she climbed into the middle of the bench seat.

"Hi, Mr. Turner."

"Hi Blanca. You look lovely." His dad backed out of the driveway and headed for the school.

They pulled up to the front of the building and for an instant the memory of the last time he'd come to a dance filled his mind. Blanca lightly touched his arm and he looked down and smiled at her. This was totally different, Gabe realized.

His father leaned down to see out the open passenger door. "I'll be waiting at the corner over there when you get out."

Gabe nodded and closed the door. Blanca looped her arm through his and they walked up the steps. Hannah sat at a table in the doorway taking tickets.

"Hi Gabe, you made it." She gave him a big smile. Joe stood behind her talking to Bobby. He turned quickly and scanned Blanca up and down.

"Introduce me to your date, Turner."

Hannah swatted him playfully. "Mind your manners."

Joe laughed.

"Hannah, Joe, this is Blanca, Blanca, Hannah and Joe."
Gabe said, gesturing to each person.

Hannah glanced around. "Hey Crystal, can you take the
door for a while?" Hannah stood and motioned them toward
the refreshment table. Joe, Bobby and Charlene joined them.
"Where do you go to school?"

"Carmel." Blanca answered.

"How'd you meet?" Charlene asked.

Blanca looked up at Gabe and hesitated for a second.
"We're on the same search team."

"Wait a minute," Hannah chimed in, "What search team?"

Blanca turned to him, her eyes big and pleading.

"Blanca, another boy, Shane, and I hide for search and
rescue dogs to help with their training. She was made a junior
handler and given a puppy today."

Blanca blushed and looked down at her toes. Gabe smiled
at her and gently patted the hand she had looped through his arm.

"Let that get out and everyone will want you on the student
council. I'm going to love running your campaign." Hannah
smiled and rubbed her hands together.

Gabe spun to face her and scowled. "That's not why I belong to the team."

"What campaign?" Blanca had stopped studying her toes
and looked back up at his face.

Hannah answered for him. "We've been trying to convince
Gabe to run for student council. Can you help us talk him into it?"

"I'd have to understand his reasons for not wanting the
position, before I consider trying to change his mind."

Hannah threw her hands up. "Great, a female version of Gabe,
just what we need." She rolled her eyes and shook her head
then reached out and hugged Blanca. "Which is a compliment."

Gabe tugged on Blanca's hand, "Let's dance." She smiled
and followed him to the dance floor.

"Why don't you want to run for student council?" Her hands
rested on his shoulders and they swayed in time to the music.

"I'm not sure, it's just I don't like all the public attention. I like helping out but I don't want to have to be running around findings ways to make people like me. It took long enough to learn to like myself."

"I don't understand."

"Long story. Maybe I'll be able to tell you about it at a search practice some day."

She nodded and leaned her head on his chest. He gave her a light hug and returned to dancing.

"Thanks, Father in Heaven," Gabe prayed.

*****

The alarm clock went off with an annoying loud ring. "Oh, I want to sleep." He rolled onto his back and laid there spread eagle. All day yesterday he'd spent running to follow his Dad's directions at yard work. Every muscle in his body ached.

I'd better hit the shower and head for church. He struggled up out of bed and limped into the bathroom then leaned back out the door. He could hear the water running in his parents' shower. What are they doing up? Is Mom coming with me?

He dashed into the bathroom and showered in a hurry. He need to clean out his truck cab if she was to ride with him. He toweled off but skipped drying his hair. He snagged his slacks, yanked on a polo shirt and made a dash for the door.

"Where are you going, in such a hurry?" His dad stood in the kitchen doorway. He was wearing a suit and tie.

"I wanted to clean out my truck before Mom got in."

"Do it after church. We're taking her car." His dad sipped a cup of coffee.

"You're going, too?"

His dad let out a sigh and put his cup down on the closest counter. "No promises that I'll stick to this, but I figured if you could find the courage to take a girl to a dance and your mom could find the courage to go to church, then it was time I stopped being the family coward."

Gabe reached over and gave his dad a big hug. Tears ran down his face but he didn't care.

His dad hugged him back and then gave him a gentle push. "Quit messing up my suit and go finish dressing. I don't plan on being late after fourteen years."

Gabe turned back toward his room and wiped his tears away with his arm.

"I'll be right there."

SCOUTING TERMS

Adult Leaders — Grown ups that assist with the business and safety of the troop. They are under the guidance and direction of the Troop Master. They do not interfere in the scouts running of the troop unless there is a safety issue or violation of the principles of scouting.

Board of Review — Before a rank advancement scouts go before a panel of adult leaders to demonstrate they have met the requirements of the new rank. For Eagle there is a review at the troop level and then the council level

Class A Shirt — The tan uniform shirt with council, troop, patrol and rank insignias worn for troop meetings and formal presentations or events

Color Guard — Scouts assigned to carry or escort the American Flag and the troop flag

Court of Honor — Gathering of troop members and their families to recognize the scouts who have achieved rank advancement

Cracker Barrel — At camp outs, generally on the first night out the scouts and leaders gather around a shared bag of snacks and talk about plans for the camp out, tell stories and jokes

Crossing over — Ceremony where boys transfer from cub scouts to boy scouts

Eagle Project — Life scouts select a project to benefit the community. The rules are strict. It must benefit the community not just the troop. For the Eagle project the scout must demonstrate the skills to direct and motive others and plan and execute the steps necessary for completion. All of this must be done by the scout, not by his parents or adult leaders

Fall In — Line up by patrols or rank and pay attention to the directions about to be given

Flag Ceremony — Sometimes called posting or retrieving the colors. The American flag must always be treated with respect recognizing that people have been injured and/or died to protect the freedoms the flag represents. It is never dipped or placed lower than any other flag nor allowed to touch the ground

KP — Kitchen Patrol doing the cooking and clean up

Merit Badges — Approximately 155 merit badges are available to the scouts. There is a merit badge booklet for each with activities to teach the scout about the subject. Some of the merit badges, such as first aid and citizenship, personal management and fitness are required for all scouts to learn. An adult leader takes on the responsibility of teaching the merit badge and must demonstrate knowledge in the field to do so.

Order of the Arrow — The service arm of the boy scouts, members act and serve as a brotherhood without thought to recognition

Patrol — A group of 5-15 boys of approximately the same rank or age that work together on camp outs and frequently on merit badges. There is a patrol structure to maintain discipline and communications.

Patrol Guide — An older/higher ranking scout that has the role of guiding the younger/less experienced scouts through merit badges, camping activities and rank advancement. The guide helps the scout learn and avoid mistakes.

Post the Colors — The troop is called to attention and scouts salute as the American flag and troop flag are carried to the front of the room and placed in stands. Usually the pledge of allegiance and Scout Law and Scout Oath are recited

Ranks — As a scout accomplishes his tasks and learning he increases in rank from lowest to highest they are: Scout, Tenderfoot, Second Class, First Class, Star, Life, Eagle, Eagle with palms. Star and Life require the scout to stay in that rank for a specified length of time. The Eagle palms are awarded to Eagle Scouts who earn additional merit badges after becoming an Eagle

Retrieve the Colors — The troop gathers by patrol and salutes while a color guard removes the American flag and troop flag. The troop leader then dismisses the members of the troop

Sash — An olive green loop of fabric worn over the right shoulder and across to the left hip. The merit badges are sewn onto the sash.

Scout Law — What a scout strives to be. A scout is trustworthy, loyal, helpful, friendly, courteous, kind, obedient, cheerful, thrifty, brave, clean, and reverent. There is also the motto "Be Prepared".

Scout oath — "On my honor I will do my best to do my duty to God and my country and to obey the Scout Law; to help other people at all times; to keep myself physically strong, mentally awake, and morally straight.

Signs up — Scouts raise their right hand in the "V" and turn to other scouts and say "signs up". They hold their hand in the air and remain silent, giving their attention to the person speaking

Topographical map — A map which shows the contours and physical features of the terrain is extensive detail, generally at the scale where 1 inch equals 2000 feet

Troop — A group of several patrols with adult leadership and chartered from the local council

Troop Leader — Scout elected or appointed to lead the entire troop and guide the planning of activities. Only adult leaders supersede his orders

Troop Master — The adult leader charged with the direction and safety of the troop. He handles the day to day activities with the support and guidance of the troop committee. He is at all meetings, camp outs and outings of the troop and bears the responsibility and the respect of all.

Webelos — "We Be Loyal Scouts". It is the transition rank in Cub Scouts where a boy and his parents investigate scout troops and starts to learn about camping out and more adult activity life skills.

RECIPES

Dump Cake
    1 can pineapple pieces
    1 can pie filling (usually cherry or blueberry)
    1 boxed cake mix (usually yellow, but can be chocolate)
    1 can 7 Up/ lemon lime soda

Preheat oven to 350 and grease a 9 x 11 cake pan. Open and drain pineapple, spread on bottom of pan. Spread pie filling over top. Sprinkle cake mix on top. Pour can of soda over top and try to spread it out. Do not stir. Place in oven and cook for approximately 30 minutes. Can also be baked in a dutch oven in coals.

Rattlesnake Pasta
    2 lbs sausage
    1- 14 oz box of pasta
    3 peppers (green, yellow, red)
    1 onion
    1 jar alfredo sauce

Sauté peppers and onions. Cut sausage into bite size pieces. Add to onions and peppers and cook thoroughly. Boil pasta, al dente, (firm but not hard.) Warm sauce. Drain pasta. Add sausage, peppers and onions. Add sauce.

Monster Cookies

(We generally make a half batch unless they are going with the boy scout troop to Ma-Ka-Ja-Wan)

- 12 eggs
- 2 lbs. brown sugar
- 4 cups white sugar
- 1 tablespoon vanilla
- 1 tablespoon corn syrup
- 8 teaspoons baking soda
- 1 lb. margarine
- 3 lbs. peanut butter
- 18 cups oatmeal
- 1 lb. M&M's
- 1 lb. Chocolate chips

Preheat oven to 350F. Cream margarine, sugar and eggs. Add vanilla, corn syrup, baking soda. Blend in peanut butter. Add M&M's, and Chocolate chips. Stir in oatmeal. Using an ice cream scoop, place 6-8 on an ungreased cookie sheet. Bake 12-15 minutes

CPSIA information can be obtained at www.ICGtesting.com
Printed in the USA
LVOW010341171011

250759LV00001B/14/P